THE SURVIVALIST 13
PURSUIT

Rourke ran down the long green mall, his
M-16 bouncing across his back on its sling.
Ahead was a tall building, and Rourke could
see green-clad men wielding swords pouring
down the steps of the building, running
toward him. They were shouting a bizarre but
beautiful sounding language.

That this was some sort of survival colony
was clear — but how they had survived? *And
who were they?*

Rourke swung the M-16 forward,
chambered a round, worked the selector to
auto, and fired into the ground a dozen yards
ahead of the men running at him.

The leaders slowed, then stopped. None of
them moved.

There was a word for it — standoff . . .

**The Survivalist series by Jerry Ahern
published by New English Library:**

The Survivalist 13
Pursuit

Jerry Ahern

NEW ENGLISH LIBRARY
Hodder and Stoughton

First published in the USA in 1986 by
Kensington Publishing Corporation

Copyright © 1986 by Jerry Ahern
NEL Paperback Edition 1987

British Library C.I.P.

Ahern, Jerry
    Pursuit.—(The Survivalist; 13)
    I. Title   II. Series
    813'.54[F]   PS3551.H4/

ISBN 0 450 40577 X

Printed and bound in Great Britain for
Hodder and Stoughton Paperbacks, a
division of Hodder and Stoughton Ltd.,
Mill Road, Dunton Green, Sevenoaks,
Kent (Editorial Office: 47 Bedford
Square, London, WC1B 3DP) by
Cox & Wyman Ltd., Reading.

For Darthy Hix — hope you enjoy this — best wishes . . .

Chapter One

The bullet crease along the left side of his ribcage was the sort of thing that would, literally, only hurt when he laughed. But John Rourke worried little over the potential for pain — for there was nothing to laugh about. Nor would there soon be. As soon as Colonel Wolfgang Mann's forces — the last of the new SS holding out in isolated, futile pockets of resistance — had consolidated their positions, Mann's replacement crew for the Complex's electronic defenses and countermeasures had discovered that a substantial force was moving on the Complex, by land and air. Mann, his broken foot being set but without painkiller, had simply said, "Soviet."

Natalia had whispered, "Vladmir."

Sarah had only sighed.

John Rourke had murmured, "Shit."

Kurinami had gone for Elaine Halversen, retrieving Sarah, Helene Sturm, her three young sons, and her newborn infant daughters.

Rourke had changed out of the black SS BDUs, into his Levis and his blue shirt, into his own combat boots as well. He had been sitting with a second cup of coffee, the first drunk while the radio communications link between Helmut Sturm and Colonel Mann had been established. With Sturm suiciding after the realization that his wife and children had nearly died at the hands of the Nazi regime he had sworn to serve, a junior officer had been given charge of the unit by Colonel Mann and they had been directed to join Dr. Munchen and the handful of German troops assisting Eden Project Base, to secure the site in the event of further Soviet attack.

While drinking the second cup of coffee, Rourke had been reloading the magazines for his pistols, checking his assault rifles, touching up the edge on his Gerber fighting knife. When the news had come of the impending Soviet attack under the leadership of Vladmir Karamatsov, Rourke had silently finished his coffee, finished the reloading of his magazines, holstered those pistols he had holsters for, sheathed his knife.

When Captain Hartman had made the announcement, Natalia had quietly asked where her things were. Frau Mann, who had joined them in the reception area near the communications center, had gone with her, Sarah joining them as had Elaine Halversen. Only Kurinami had sat with Rourke. When Rourke stood, Akiro Kurinami stood, his voice low as he asked, "Do we fight, John?"

"Yes," Rourke had told the Japanese naval lieutenant, then started from the communications center. It hadn't taken long to find Colonel Mann, on crutches, his officers surrounding him, in the Complex street outside the communications center. Mann had seen Rourke, signaling to him and Kurinami, who had walked toward the knot of officers, the officers parting like a wave to give Rourke and the young Japanese access to Mann. "Colonel," Rourke almost whispered.

"You have fought this man before. Do you have any suggestions?"

"He might be the devil," Rourke said slowly. "But he's flesh and blood. He wants to live. He's committed more to himself than to his cause — but they may be one and the same. If we can show him he'll be in personal danger, he'll take a considerable portion of his force with him, leave a rear guard, and flee to fight another day."

"A lightning commando strike to the heart of his forces, then."

"Yes," Rourke nodded slowly.

"Perhaps more easily said than done, Dr. Rourke. A third of the personnel available to defend the Complex were either loyal to the Leader and are since dead, or wounded or under guard. Or fighting for freedom. But a full third of the potential force here is unable to fight. Considerable equipment has been damaged."

Rourke took one of the thin, dark tobacco cigars from the inside breast pocket of the brown bomber jacket. "Give me a few men and some equipment. I'll lead a raid into Karamatsov's field HQ if we can pinpoint it. At the same time I strike, cut a wedge in his front lines with the biggest counterattack force you can muster without leaving the Complex defenseless. Make him think we're stronger than we are. Put him in fear of his life."

And Rourke heard the voice behind him. "I'm going with you." It was Natalia.

Rourke looked away from Mann, toward Natalia. She stood silhouetted against the street, the street a bustle of military activity, armed men running, assault rifles at high port, military vehicles moving up toward the Complex's main entrance. "You and Sarah and Elaine — the three of you can stay here, help with the defense of the Complex. I'll take Akiro if he wants to come."

"I will come," Kurinami said quickly, enthusiastically.

"I will come," Natalia whispered, just as firmly, but

her voice flat, lifeless-sounding. "I know my husband, how he thinks, better than anyone. If we each go, we can split your penetration team into two elements perhaps twice the chance of success of catching Vladmir by surprise." Her hands rested on the flaps of her holsters. She had changed into her usual fighting gear—a black jumpsuit that looked sensual on her despite its utility; nearly-knee-high black low-heeled boots; her black canvas bag, which converted from purse to daypack, hanging suspended from her left shoulder; an M-16 slung cross-body, muzzle down along her back, its muzzle and flash suppressor just barely visible from where he watched her; the silenced American Walther PPK/S in the shoulder holster under her left arm, inverted, the silencer tube muzzle up. Her almost-black hair rested against her shoulders and she tossed her head, a stray lock of the hair falling across her forehead, into her eyes, the surrealistic blue of her eyes hard somehow, set.

"All right," he told her.

The minitanks of the Germans reminded Rourke of stories heard of Rommel utilizing cardboard tanks placed over Volkswagens to make his Allied enemies assume the Desert Fox had greater reserves of armor than he actually possessed. The minitanks were little larger than Volkswagens, one-man units, the weapons systems operated electronically by the driver. Aside from the integrity of the armor which was obvious, they were little more than one-man wheeled body armor.

Captain Hartman had assigned a Sergeant Hofsteader to give both Rourke and Natalia and Kurinami a short course. "Herr Doctor, Fräulein Major, Herr Lieutenant. To fully utilize the KP-6 one must spend several weeks in training, utilizing simulators and then actual field trials. But the KP-6 can be driven from one place to another as simply as an automobile. Utilizing the weapons systems while the vehicle is in motion without upsetting the vehicle itself is the difficult part, as are quick turns and reverses. I am a student of antique armor, Herr Doctor. Just as in your days, when tanks were likely to throw or break a tread and become disabled, the KP-6 is likely to overturn if not handled properly. With an experienced operator at the controls, the vehicles are almost impossible to overturn, even if firing while turning. So—you have been warned of the potential danger," Hofsteader smiled. "Fräulein Major—perhaps you would climb inside."

Natalia nodded, Rourke helping her to clamber up the side of the treaded desert-tan minitank. Hofsteader—graying, his face pale complected, his eyes a piercing china blue—climbed the opposite side, opening the hatch cover for her. Natalia twisted around, her legs down the hatch, her body sliding inside, her voice peculiarly echoing. "This is very small, Sergeant."

"Yes, Fräulein Major—but you will feel adequately comfortable once you have secured yourself into the control seat."

"Yes—I see what you mean—there's even decent leg room."

"The yoke in front of you controls side-to-side motion, as would the steering wheel of a truck. The right foot controls acceleration with the pedal to the far right, braking with the pedal to the center. The third pedal—"

"A clutch?"

Hofsteader laughed aloud. "No, Fräulein Major. The clutch . . . I have read of these, inspected these in some vehicles preserved for their historic value—but the pedal on the left is the transmission. When you

11

activate the pedal while the machine is moving forward, it automatically reverses the direction of the four main drive wheels. When you activate the pedal while in reverse, you automatically go forward. When starting the vehicle, the readout on the control panel will indicate what the gear is, forward or reverse."

Kurinami looked at Hofsteader. "Sergeant—is there no lower gear for more difficult terrain?"

"Herr Lieutenant—such is not needed. Sensors located through the undercarriage of the machine and within the treads themselves constantly monitor the terrain and self-compensate."

"How can you shift at speed—straight from forward into reverse—without stripping gears?" Rourke inquired.

"Forward drive and reverse are totally separate units. Activating the pedal trips out of one drive into another."

"You must lay down a lot of rubber," Rourke smiled.

Hofsteader only smiled, apparently not understanding the term, Rourke thought—but there was no time to elaborate. Hofsteader began explaining the functions of each major readout and button and switch. Cruising speed of the minitank was, translated from kilometers into miles, eighty per hour, top speed on level dry terrain ninety-six miles per hour. Totally amphibious, it could climb dry obstacles with a 70-degree angle from the horizontal. Mounted atop the vehicle was a repeating 40mm grenade launcher with the capability of turreting a full 360 degrees while in firing mode or on search. Mounted on each side of the tank were missile launchers, the missiles targeted through a gunsight targeting computer on the control console behind which Natalia sat. Three missiles on each side. To the front and rear were twin, independently targetable machine guns—about .70 caliber, Rourke judged—giving the driver the capability of firing in four different directions at once if needed.

He glanced at the Rolex on his wrist — in another ten minutes, the counterattack force would be assembled, his own commando unit assembled. The Russians would strike at any moment as indicated in the last report from the electronic defenses and countermeasures unit. Hofsteader broke his monology — "Are there any questions? Comments? Gentlemen? Fräulein Major?"

Kurinami laughed. "If this were five centuries ago, my country could have made it cheaper and with greater fuel economy."

Rourke realized he had been both right and wrong — right that his left ribcage would only hurt when he laughed and wrong that there would be no reason to laugh. He laughed. His ribcage hurt . . .

Krakovski sat at the controls of his machine. The Hero Colonel, Karamatsov, was now a marshal. There would be promotions, at least one colonelcy to be had this day, Krakovski told himself. Either Antonovitch, one of the Hero Marshal's Elite, or himself, from the new generations bred for warfare within the Underground City in the Urals.

Krakovski intended that it should be himself rather than Antonovitch.

He spoke into his headset microphone. "This is Krakovski. At the appointed moment, one thought must be uppermost in your minds, my comrades. We do not fight against these Nazis and their capitalist allies for personal glory, we fight for the security of the Soviet people, for World Communism. No more noble cause exists, and in this cause, no sacrifice is too great. For some of us, this may prove our last moment together. The Nazi stronghold is well fortified. But, it cannot withstand our combined efforts, the collective will to victory. And victory is the only alternative, comrades." It was something that if the battle went well would be remembered. "Victory is the only alternative." If a statue were erected to him, it would be the perfect inscription.

His diary—he would note it there, save it. He began increasing the revolutions of his main rotor, watching the instruments as temperatures rose into the accepted levels. "Victory is the only alternative." It had a nice sound to it, Major Krakovski thought, rolling it silently on his tongue . . .

Vladmir Karamatsov looked at his watch. The sun should rise soon, and with the sunrise his forces would attack out of the east, against the Nazi stronghold. He paced away from the hastily erected village of tents that would serve as his temporary headquarters, the sounds of the waiting gunships like the sounds of insects swarming, ready to strike if provoked. The world had provoked this, he thought within himself. The world had provoked its own destruction, in its failure to relent to the inexorable. Good. Evil. The words meant little to him, one man's good another man's evil. There was no truth to quest for—truth was subjective, within the mind of the seeker.

He had found his truth—the acquisition of personal power, and a greater truth still—revenge. His loins ached with it. Natalia—he had just begun to punish her and Rourke had taken her from him again. Karamatsov flexed his arm where he had sustained the recent bullet wound. The next time—he would kill Natalia slowly, in inconceivable agony, and whether he killed Rourke by his own hand would then be immaterial—because Rourke loved her, and when she died so horribly, Rourke's soul would die.

He stopped at the far perimeter of the clearing in which the tents had been set, the predawn air warm, moist. There was life here — this time, this life which had been snatched from death at Rourke's hands — but if for some reason there was not total victory, then there would be total destruction.

He had arranged that, would exercise that option if it were the last remaining option.

There had been men throughout history who had striven for the ultimate control, the power of life and death over the world as it was known in their times. And if he, Marshal Vladmir Karamatsov, could not have the power of life, then he would exercise his power of death and it would be the ultimate power, the irresistible power.

Soon it would be sunrise. Soon the battle would start.

Chapter Two

The horizon to the east was a line of luminescent grey as Rourke took Sarah into his arms and held her. A wind—warm, damp—buffeted the helipad complex atop the mountain into which the Complex had been built five centuries ago, the hissing and thwacking of rotor blades cutting the jungle air only heightening the sense of unreality. "We'll be all right here," Sarah said into his right ear, Rourke feeling her breath on his skin. "But you—and Natalia and Akiro—be careful. Please. Come back to me, John. I feel something. And I know it's silly. But I feel something inside of me. Like I felt when Michael was inside me, when I carried Annie. It's—ahh—"

Rourke held his wife closely. "I feel it too. I'm sorry—about what I did with Michael and Annie, using the cryogenic process to let them grow up. But I did what I thought was best for all of us to survive—them especially."

"I know that," she answered, Rourke's eyes focused in her hair—she still smelled of expensive perfume, just a little, the smell lingering from the masquerade they had carried out in order to rescue Frau Sturm and her children. She had changed clothes—black slacks, a gray sleeveless cotton sweater. "If I am—well, pregnant—I, ahh—I didn't try to get you to get me pregnant—just to—well—because of Natalia."

"I know that," he told her. "I love you—always have. Maybe we'll make this work out." He touched his fingertips to the tip of her chin, raising her face, brushing his lips against hers, then kissing her harder, his arms tight around her. "Be careful yourself," he told her, then released her, catching up his assault rifle from the pavement, not looking back, breaking into a run for the minitank, clambering aboard, setting the M-16 across the top of the turret, lowering himself feet first into the cockpit of the minitank, reaching up for the rifle. He looked along the field—Kurinami's minitank, Kurinami closing the hatch. Natalia—she was dropping through—shot him a wave. He looked the entire length of the mountaintop field—beside Kurinami's, Natalia's, and his own machine, eighteen others, each hitched on a cable lead, the lead running to the fuselage undercarriage of one of the German helicopters. It was a procedure Mann had invented and practiced with his pilots to perfection, Captain Hartman had told Rourke: Air-mobile, rapid-deployment armor to any portion of a battlefield that could be reached by helicopter gunship; the weight of the minitanks, despite the efficacy of their armor, light; the gunships able to travel at combat speeds when necessary, to hover over the battlefield, lower the minitanks into the battlefield and cover the tanks with guns and missiles until the tanks were freed of the hauling harnesses and could defend themselves.

He had been told to watch for signs of nausea, since the tanks would sway badly at times.

He had eaten nothing.

He stared back across the field—Sarah, gray sweater, black slacks, gunbelt at her waist. John Rourke wondered if there would ever be peace. He didn't wave. He looked. Sarah looked back. He nodded, tucked down and closed the lid of the tank, adjusting his body mass into the contours of the pilot's seat, the minitanks not built for someone with his leg length, but making the best of it as he found the harness closures and started to buckle in, his eyes already scanning the control console readouts. But his eyes left the console, glanced to the Rolex Submariner on his left wrist — it was dawn . . .

Col. Wolfgang Mann stood before the upper battlements of the Complex, staring down across the meticulously manicured lands that surrounded it, lands reclaimed from devastation, replanted to aid nature, now to be fertilized with the blood of men. Warfare had been much different when studied in the abstraction, when practiced in the abstraction that there really was no enemy out there. But it had all become suddenly different.

Young Helmet Sturm had taken his own life because of it. Men and women had died in battle now. The Leader and his faithful SS, many, like the Leader, dead, some at their own hands, others more honorably in combat. And there would be executions, he realized — those among the SS who had caused the innocent murders of others, plotted the death of Dieter Bern and the ensuing purge there would have been.

The voice of Dieter Bern — philosopher, teacher, scientist, and now the new leader — echoed from the loudspeaker system, across the battlements and the airfield they surrounded, down the mountainside, to the ground troops and tanks deployed below. "This night we have won our freedom from tyranny — and so soon our resolve is tested. The fight of good men against evil is, perhaps, never ended. There will be glory, there will be misery, there will be moments filled with the rapture of courage, moments of unutterable agony. Right. Wrong. They are in the hearts and minds of men, not some abstraction which can be reached for, examined, analyzed. We fight for freedom. Our enemies fight to kill or enslave us. We fight the good fight. That is all that can be asked, and our finest sacrifice. The hopes and aspirations of us all go with you into battle."

The voice echoed away, ended on the wind.

His foot ached, but the pain was steady since it had been set, no longer all-but-uncontrollable spasms of pain. He withstood it. The radio crackled and he spoke into his headset. "Yes, Captain Hartman."

"Herr Colonel — the assault force awaits your command."

Wolfgang Mann closed his eyes. This God some of the Americans had spoken of, that he had read of in banned books — he wondered if this God would take his prayer at face value, if this God indeed existed. "God — bless them," he murmured.

"Herr Colonel?"

"Hartman — my prayers are with you. Attack."

"Yes, Herr Colonel!"

Wolfgang Mann felt the wind suddenly die . . .

Through the viewport — with the viewport, Rourke corrected himself, because there was no actual window — the terrain was viewed by means of two 180-degree scanning television-type cameras, monitoring front- or rearview at the flick of a control switch. Rourke scanned forward, punching on the overhead scan now as well — the air seemed alive with fighter aircraft and gunships, the bursts of aerial mortars and the contrails of rockets everywhere. The attack against the Complex had begun when Rourke had expected, but its pace was quicker than he had imagined it could have been. Fighters screened the gunships that ferried them across the battlefield, but the hull of the minitank rang with the impact of machine gun fire, rocked with the nearby airbursts of the mortars, Rourke clutching the armrests of his seat now, powerless to aid himself. If the gunship that ferried the minitank should take a hit, he would be dead.

The reality of death was something he had faced more times than he could remember or chose to recall—but never a powerless death like this. He thought of Natalia in her minitank, of Kurinami in his. They all shared the same potential fate. And if the gunships reached behind Karamatsov's lines successfully, the minitanks would only be set into the heart of the battlefield, albeit from the rear.

A rocket detonated nearby, Rourke's ears ringing with the concussion the blast imparted to his tank, the tank swaying violently on its pendulum chain, Rourke scanning above. The gunship smoked. "Holy shit," Rourke hissed, locking his fists tighter to the chair arms. He scanned ahead, ground forces, tanks backed by infantry, closing against one another, like some battle of Armageddon. He hit the scan switch, scanning rearward now, the gray sky dark with smoke, images of fighter aircraft dogfighting over the Complex. Sarah, he thought, almost verbalizing the name.

He glanced to the overhead monitor again—smoke had turned to fire, the German gunship's fuselage tail section licking flames, Rourke inhaling, tensing his neck muscles, his mind racing for alternatives, his eyes scanning the forward monitor again, working the switch to forward view. Soviet infantry was beneath him, but he was behind the line of tanks that spearheaded their advance. He could hear the pilot of the helicopter on his comlink through the headphones.

"Herr Doctor Rourke—my machine—it is going out of control. I am wounded—dying."

"Get to the ground—I'll get to you."

"No—there is a better way. I will hover, release the KP-6, Herr Doctor—I am dying anyway."

"What do you mean a better way, Lieutenant?" He didn't even know the boy's name.

But there was no answer—only static, Rourke feeling it in his stomach as the minitank began to descend. He heard the voice of the young officer again. "On ten, Herr Doctor—I shall release at the count of ten. There will be heavy small-arms fire, but placing you in their midst will preclude use of antitank weapons. Make certain your hatch lock is secure, Herr Doctor."

Rourke started to speak, but only the static again—he glanced up to the control panel; the hatch lock was secure. He manually confirmed that, reaching up. He checked the controls on the panel, powering the KP-6 up, wasting fuel, but it was synthetic anyway, abundant.

He scanned his rear—the other helicopters were following suit, starting to descend, to place the KP-6 minitanks of Natalia and Akiro Kurinami and the eighteen volunteers from among Wolfgang Mann's troops into the center of the battlefield. He scanned forward—small-arms fire in heavy concentration, a mortar crew taking position. He had no idea whether the Soviet mortars were powerful enough to stop the minitank and neither did the Germans who had armored the KP-6.

"Ten," the voice of the young pilot began, a deathly quality to it already. "Nine. Eight. Seven. Six. Five. Four. Three. Two. One—luck to you, Herr Doctor!" Rourke felt the sway, the lurch, heard the release of the lock above, the tank dropping slightly as Rourke worked the extreme left pedal, the minitank impacting, bouncing, jarring, Rourke feeling it in his bones, in his teeth, working the far right pedal, accelerating, cutting the wheel, trying not to cut too sharp—right, aiming the minitank for the mortar emplacement, infantrymen of the KGB force assaulting the minitank, clambering onto it. He hit the control button for external electrical charge, electrifying the skin of the tank, the forward monitor and the overhead monitor showing the lightning-bolt twists of electricity flickering between the minitank's shell and the men who had clambered over her, the men falling away, clothing and flesh smoking. Rourke hit the power off—he had been told it was a direct drain on the batteries. The mortar emplacement was coming close now, Rourke activating his missile targeting system, locking the right side missile bank onto the mortar plate and the crew surrounding it, hitting the fire switch, the minitank rocking slightly, a thudding sound, then the missile's contrail appearing in his forward screen. There was a flash of brilliant light, a belching ball of upward-rising smoke and flame, the mortar emplacement gone. Rourke hit for rear scan—he could see the flaming gunship, aiming itself toward the concentration of tanks at the center of the forward battle line. Rourke whispered, "No."

The helicopter—it was there one instant, the tail section consumed with flame—and then a massive fireball engulfed the helicopter and the four tanks nearest it, secondary explosions now, the ground beneath the minitank rocking with them. And in his ears, he heard Kurimani's voice, a whisper, "We called them the Divine Wind—it is the same."

Rourke closed his eyes for an instant, blindly hitting the forward scan, opening his eyes. "Natalia—with me?"

"I'm okay, John."

"Akiro—all in one piece?"

"At least."

Rourke smiled. "Strike force—sound off!"

Numbers rang in Rourke's ears: one, two, three, four—through eighteen, all eighteen of the volunteer force on the ground, mobile.

"Akiro—left flank. Natalia—right flank. My men—follow me—remember, save those skin charges. Batteries die, they tell me."

They were almost all officers who commanded the minitanks, officers and a few senior noncoms, all of them chosen not only for their abilities but for their English, no time for a command in the heat of battle to be lost in translation or to Rourke's adequate but not perfect German. Kurinami spoke the language not at all. Only Natalia had what Rourke considered perfect fluency, even the perfect accent.

Infantry surrounded them now. Rourke piloted the KP-6 minitank ahead, firing his machine guns, spraying into the enemy forces, but holding back with the turret-mounted 40mm grenade launcher—he was saving it for Karamatsov's headquarters.

"John—aircraft coming in low—fighter." It was Natalia. "He's opening fire."

"Evasive action," Rourke ordered, cutting the wheel hard right—not too hard he hoped—then back left, zigzagging, hitting to rear scan, the ground behind him furrowing with lines of machine gun fire. The tank rocked as a rocket impacted some fifty yards behind him. Rourke swung the turret rearward 180 degrees, punching the targeting button, the 40mm grenade launcher's targeting frame appearing on his screen, following, tracking the incoming fighter as it began a second pass. "Stay clear of me," Rourke hissed into his headset microphone, centering the targeting frame over the fuselage underbelly—he hit the fire-control button, zigzagging the tank again as the ground behind him began to ripple once more with machine-gun fire, the fighter plane exploding, chunks of fuselage and wing bursting outward, the airspace it had filled a split second before now nothing but flames. The minitank rocked, the shell reverberating with the impacts of debris from the fighter aircraft.

Rourke hit to forward scan, cutting the wheel hard left just in time, avoiding impact with a jeep-like vehicle mounted with a recoilless rifle, working the controls for the turret-mounted grenade launcher, working the target-acquisition frame, settling the frame over the center of the jeep-like gun carrier, hitting fire control—the vehicle vaporizing into a ball of flame, Rourke working the turret full forward now— he would save the rest of the grenades for Karamatsov's HQ.

He put the machine gun on automatic scatterfire, the machine guns twisting crazily—unpredictably, it seemed as he viewed them—working from front to rear and back to forward, the machine guns covering the area around the KP-6 with a curtain of fire.

More infantry ahead—and spearheading them, a full-sized Soviet tank.

"John—do you see that—on your right?"

"I see it, Akiro—get away from it—we can outmaneuver it." At least Sergeant Hofsteader had told them that, Rourke recalled, cutting his steering yoke left, the tank bouncing and jarring over the grassy terrain, infantry fleeing before him, the Soviet tank—the size of an Abrams or larger—altering course, coming for him.

Rourke spoke into his headset. "If this guy has our frequency, we're dead meat. . . . All right, listen everybody. Even numbers take the tank's right tread, odd

24

numbers take the left. Use the turret-mounted grenade launchers. When I count down, acquire, and when I say fire, do it. On my mark—from five—Five! Four! Three!" Rourke settled his own targeting frame at the underbelly side of the left tread. "Two! One! *Fire!*"

The minitanks he could see in the peripheral edges of the forward scan fired, streaks of white smoke propellant converging on the treads of the giant Soviet tank, impacting, smoke and dust momentarily obscuring the tank, then fireballs erupting on either side of it, the machine rocking, seeming for a moment to be airborne, then crashing downward.

The screams in his ears from the strike force—the momentary victory.

"Let's cut out that infantry," Rourke rasped, cutting his yoke right, cutting back left, compensating as he felt the machine start to tip. He accelerated out of it, the minitank jumping a large hummock of earth, bouncing, his machine guns scatter-firing, the Soviet infantry falling away.

Tents in the distance. Natalia's voice through his headset. "John—it must be Vladmir's HQ."

Rourke whispered into the microphone. "Let's get him!" Boosting his acceleration, Rourke armed another missile, setting the targeting frame for the missile in his forward console, settling the bulls-eye over the farthest of the tents, hitting fire control. The minitank rocked, the thudding sound against the skin, the contrail, the impact, a fireball bursting skyward, parts of men and equipment scattered in its wake. Natalia's team to his right—they were moving out in a flanking maneuver, Rourke speaking into his headset. "Numbers thirteen through eighteen—up the middle—come on. Akiro—your team—"

"Flanking left," the voice cut back.

Rourke targeted another missile, firing, the bank on

the right side of the tank empty, targeting another missile, firing, two tents going up this time along with a helicopter near them.

He switched to the 40mm grenade launcher mounted on the turret, swinging the turret in a wide arc, acquiring a target—another Soviet chopper. He fired, the chopper vaporizing.

Running men, with infantry guarding their withdrawal, Rourke heading his KP-6 straight at them, his forward machine guns now the only ones firing, but scatterfire still, mowing the Soviet soldiers down, then he was targeting another missile beyond them, toward the running men, firing, another helicopter starting airborne, men on the ground near it, all consumed in the fireball.

One missile remained.

To his right—Natalia's force was engaging another tank. Dead ahead—he could see a knot of infantry running, a helicopter swaying slightly as though about to go airborne instantly. Inside him, he felt it, knew it—"Karamatsov." He started the KP-6 toward him.

"John—we're in trouble." Natalia's voice. Rourke hit to reverse scan, two of the KP-6s under Natalia's command smoldering balls of twisted metal, a fireball puffing skyward. The tank. It was firing again, another of the minitanks gone.

"Akiro—cut right—help Natalia."

"On the way."

Rourke hit for forward scan, the helicopter nearer now, men running to it as infantrymen fell into prone positions, firing toward him. An RPG-like device at the shoulder of a kneeling man. There was no choice— Rourke swerved to avoid the rocket, the ground beside him shaking, the sound of shrapnel impacting the skin of the minitank. Rourke watched as the fusilier loaded another missile, swinging it to Rourke's right. Natalia.

26

Rourke settled his last missile on the man with the RPG, firing, the man and the men around him gone in a black and orange fireball.

The helicopter—it was starting airborne, men climbing to its skids, Rourke firing the 40mm grenade-launching device on the turret, grenades exploding on both sides of the chopper, the chopper visibly buffeted by the explosions, but still climbing.

Akiro's voice. "John—this is a different kind of tank—the treads must be armored. We're not stopping it."

Rourke whispered, "Later," but not to Akiro—to the man he knew was inside the fleeing chopper.

He hit for rear scan—the tank was closing on Natalia's forces, two tanks with her, Akiro's force coming up on the tank's right flank. Rourke spoke into his headset. "My team—clean up here. Wipe out the headquarters," and then hit for forward scan, slowing the KP-6, starting the minitank into a wide arc to his right, recovering the yoke, accelerating—the Soviet tank was firing again, two of Akiro's force incinerated, a third tank visibly disabled.

Rourke stomped the KP-6's accelerator. Reaching to his right—the M-16 he had taken with him.

He caught up the assault rifle in his right fist, slamming the butt against the accelerator, wedging the flash-suppressed muzzle against the seat's right-side armrest—the length was almost tailor-made.

Rourke punched the release for his seat restraint, hitting the hatch control lock on the panel, the sound of the lock popping overhead.

Rourke started up from his seat, reaching to the hatch-lock handle, twisting, glancing to his monitor—the Soviet tank was perhaps two hundred yards away, the KP-6 rocking, bumping toward it at top speed. Rourke pushed up on the hatch, the slipstream tearing at his face as he pushed his head through, his eyes squinting against the dust carried on the slipstream.

His fists balled as he pushed himself free and rolled, his legs springing him away from the turret, his body impacting the ground hard, rolling, his right shoulder taking it, pain. To his feet. He stumbled, fell to his knees, looked back—fifty yards until impact. To his feet—Rourke ran, counting it off, seconds to impact. When he hit five, he threw himself down, his arms rising to shield his head and neck, the roar like a hundred thunderclaps now, the ground trembling under him.

He rolled onto his back—a fireball was rising almost lazily, flames consuming both the minitank and the Russian monster. Men were starting to clamber from the hatch of the Soviet tank, but machine-gun fire cut them down.

Rourke stood, both of the Scoremasters from his belt into his fists—but there was no fighting near him now, the sky to the east filled with retreating Soviet air-power.

Chapter Three

He had walked the battlefield, Natalia beside him, the Russian dead vastly outnumbering the German dead. A Russian soldier — a boy — had been crawling toward his weapon, using only his feet, Rourke kicking the assault rifle away, then dropping to his knees beside the boy to see if he could aid him. But the boy was dying, Natalia speaking soothingly to him in Russian.

She had asked him, "Where do you come from, Corporal?"

"The City — the Underground City. Are you the one?"

"The one?"

"Whom the Hero Marshal wants to see dead."

"He is a marshal now — Vladmir? Vladmir Karamatsov?"

The boy had nodded only, coughing, flecks of blood appearing on his chin, Natalia wiping them away — the boy's hands held in his intestines. Rourke wondered clinically how the boy would have held a gun if he had ever reached it.

"Where is the Underground City?" Rourke asked, the Russian coming to him after long disuse.

The boy either didn't hear or didn't want to answer.

"All of us — we trained for this day, when we would defeat our enemies."

"How many of you are there in the Underground City?" Rourke asked.

"The Urals — they are so beautiful."

"Do you have a girl?" Natalia asked.

"Yes — she is —" His eyes, the lids all the way back, the eyes themselves suddenly looking at nothing. Rourke closed the eyes. Natalia kissed the boy's forehead and gently lowered his head to the ground.

Kurinami had come running up. Word from Dr. Munchen. During the Nazi attack, Forrest Blackburn had proven to be the Soviet agent, kidnapped Annie by helicopter. Paul and Michael and Madison were in pursuit by truck.

"I need a helicopter," Rourke had said slowly.

Kurinami answered. "Colonel Mann has dispatched one — fighters are waiting to take us back to Eden Base, and Dr. Munchen will have helicopters fueled and ready with reserve fuel supplies, food. Colonel Mann ordered him to commandeer additional ammunition for our weapons. A helicopter will be here in minutes to take us back to the Complex. Sarah and Elaine are already waiting."

"Annie," Rourke whispered, staring skyward . . .

John Thomas Rourke studied the whiteness beyond the black shadow of the German helicopter, Natalia Anastasia Tiemerovna beside him in the copilot's seat, Sarah his wife, taking the open side door of the fuselage, a large bandage on her left forearm all that spoke of the flesh wound she had sustained. Sarah couldn't fly, Natalia could — hence Natalia sat beside him, Sarah using the binoculars to scan beyond what was possible for peripheral vision within the confines of the cockpit.

"John! I see something to your left!"

Rourke shouted back to his wife. "All right, hang on!" He started banking the machine to port, his eyes squinting behind the dark-lensed aviator-style sunglasses he habitually wore, his teeth clamped tight on the thin, dark tobacco cigar, the cigar unlit. Without the aid of the Bushnells his wife used, he could see the faint etching of tire treads in the snow now. "I see the treads," he shouted back.

Beside him, Natalia shouted—they used no headsets—"John—that dot—that black dot on the snowfield! There!"

Rourke increased rotor speed—he had been barely above stall for the last half-hour, the blowing snow beneath them having drifted over the tire tracks they had spotted hours earlier. "Hang on again, Sarah—I'm taking her down." Rourke brought the machine out of the bank, starting to descend, the dark spot taking more definite shape now—a pickup truck. His pickup truck. Michael. Madison. Paul. In search of Annie. He picked up his radio headset. "Kurinami—this is Rourke—over."

"John—Akiro here. Do you see them? Over."

"Actuating my tracking signal now." Rourke hit the toggle switch that would start the radio signal. "We see them. Rourke out."

Rourke increased speed, Sarah shouting forward, "The pickup's hood is up."

Rourke felt the tendons in his neck hardening, tightening—there was no sign of the Russian helicopter Forrest Blackburn had stolen, used to kidnap Rourke's daughter Annie. He put down the radio headset. The chance that somehow his son Michael, Madison who carried Michael's child, and his friend Paul had successfully closed with Blackburn, recovered

31

Annie—the chance was slimming to a reality of nonexistence, he knew.

Bleak, like the landscape they covered.

The black shadow of the German helicopter seemed to race ahead, forever tantalizing out of reach of the machine. But the black dot that was the truck was gaining each instant in resolution, the woodland camouflage pattern obvious against the white of the snow. The snow that had fallen throughout the early morning was still falling now, blowing in great white clouds as Rourke glanced back, icy spicules blown wavelike in the helicopter's wake.

Beside him, he heard the bolt of Natalia's M-16 being worked. Rourke reached under the left side of his battered brown bomber jacket, ripping one of the twin stainless Detonics .45s from the double Alessi shoulder rig, leaving the hammer down, putting the gun beneath his right thigh, starting to bring the chopper down.

Sarah shouted over the roar of the slipstream through the open fuselage door. "I see Paul, John—he's waving to us." Rourke's breath steamed as he exhaled, his flesh cold—from the temperature of the open aircraft and from trepidation.

Rourke too could now see the stick figure beside the truck, too far for accurate observation with the naked eye. But if Paul was waving, signaling to the helicopter, then at the least Paul was alive. Rourke's hands seemed to have a mind of their own, wanting to throttle out, but his mind controlled his hands and he held at a safe speed.

Annie—if Blackburn had harmed her—he licked his lips, starting the machine into a wide pass over the truck, as he banked toward the truck now seeing the figure beside it—Paul, his face turning away from the swirling rage of snow that was engulfing the pickup, and inside the cab, he could see Madison, Michael as well.

"I see them," Sarah shouted.

"But—"

Rourke looked at Natalia, closing his eyes once, then started out of the loop, letting the helicopter spin on its axis a full 180 degrees as he started touching down, the snow obscuring everything around them now—but no Annie.

The helicopter lurched once and glided forward and settled, Rourke punching the release for his seat restraint, Natalia doing the same. Sarah was already jumping clear as Rourke ducked his head, moving quickly along the length of the fuselage, Natalia jumping out—Paul ran to the women, Sarah hugging him, then running from him toward the opening door of the pickup's cab, Natalia embracing Paul, kissing him.

Rourke jumped to the snow, his little Detonics going from his right fist into the right hip pocket of his Levis. Natalia stepped away, Paul turning to face him. "John—we couldn't find her—tracks where it landed, stayed a while, then footprints. We followed them and lost them. We did a pattern search, found another landing spot—and a hole—" Rourke's eyes tightened at the corners. "He's dug something up—Michael theorized some kind of weapons cache or survival gear left before the Night of the War for him."

"How many sets of footprints?"

"Just one—a man's . . ."

Rourke looked into the snow at his feet, shaking his head. He raised his face, took a step forward, and embraced Paul Rubenstein. "We'll find her—so help me God."

Blackburn had kept the Soviet helicopter airborne

throughout the night and the following day—and Annie Rourke had neither closed her eyes nor spoken throughout the night, nodding off in the warmth of the sunlight when it had come. Blackburn's right hand had sometimes come to rest on her still-bare left thigh during the night. She had felt her kidneys would burst, but to have asked him to stop the machine and touch her, to undo her bonds, might have invited what her greatest immediate fear had been to come true. He had let her urinate while he had stored his long-buried cache of supplies but watched her across his gun barrel. She had barely been able to do it. And that had been a half-day ago.

The tightly sealed fuselage of the helicopter smelled faintly of gasoline—the hermetically sealed cans still unopened that filled the rear of the aircraft not the cause, but rather the half-filled can remaining from Blackburn's gassing of the helicopter at the site where his survival gear and weapons had been buried. She had tried to calculate airspeed versus time to get an approximate idea of position as they had flown. They had crossed a great body of water, either a large lake or a bay of some sort, and when dawn had come, the whitecapped water had given way to vast snowfields over which they had since been flying for what seemed like hours.

Blackburn finally spoke to her. "I'm setting down—time to refuel again. I'll untie you so you can piss and fix us some food. Don't do anything stupid, Annie. We're almost at seventy degrees north latitude on the eastern coastline of Greenland. Ice and snow—not a thing else. No one lives here anymore. Ahead of us, a hop to Iceland—we'll stay the night there and then cross into the Scandinavian Peninsula. I need some sleep. But there'll be no help for you—nothing at all." The helicopter was starting down. She looked at him—

34

his dark eyes, the smile on his lips, his voice coming through her headset microphone. "If by some quirk of fate you were able to kill me, Annie, you couldn't know how to fly a helicopter. So all you'd be doing is sentencing yourself to freeze to death here or die of exposure. If you tried flying the chopper, you'd crash and burn to death—if you were lucky."

The helicopter settled, Blackburn wrenching open his door—the icy blast of wind across the snow made her involuntarily shiver, her head aching with lack of sleep and not urinating, and now the cold racking her body. He slammed the door closed, her naked thighs goosebumped. After retying her, the first refueling finished, again he had bared the lower half of her body. Blackburn walked around the front of the helicopter, stopping beside her door, wrenching it open, the cold again, the wind.

His hands rested on her naked thighs—his hands were colder than the cold—"You remember what I said now—and what I told you before, Annie. Tonight—you'll be good, you'll want me—if you don't, well, maybe I won't take you to the Underground City and let them play with you. Maybe I'll just leave you—in Iceland. Take your coat—take your boots—it'd only take you a few hours to die, but it'd go on forever," and he smiled, reaching up, wresting the headset from her, the teardrop-shaped microphone hitting the tip of her nose, the headpiece catching in her hair, tearing some strands out, tears involuntarily flooding her eyes.

He undid the bonds at her ankles, at her hands, then released the safety harness. He stepped back, Annie trying to move her fingers—with the sides of her stiff hands forcing her skirt down over her legs. The wind howled, snow blowing, but like tiny needles of ice, stinging her cheeks, the backs of her hands, the sensation seeming to revive her hands. She began

35

moving her legs, a little, the movement only making the desire to urinate all that much more intense, her feet tingling as if asleep. Pain. He climbed past her—her eyes saw the bayonet on his equipment belt, but her fingers—she tried to flex them—she could not reach out for it. And he was right—if she killed him now, she would be trapped here and die. She couldn't fly the aircraft—she had watched him closely, but knew enough about flying to know that watching wasn't enough. And wind currents would be tricky here, engine temperatures critical.

She could hear him moving the containers of gasoline, the smell of the gasoline more intense. She licked her dry lips, saying, "I need to go to the bathroom."

He laughed, saying, "Well, I don't think you'll find one out here. Have to do it outside again—and don't get your legs too wet this time," and he laughed again. "Might be cold later. Might freeze," and he laughed once more. "Don't go too far—in this blowing snow, visibility could go in seconds."

"I know that," she whispered, moving her legs, reaching out to the open doorframe, drawing her hand back as it touched metal. The gloves in the pocket of her coat. She pulled her coat around her, buttoning it, easing up in the seat, getting her panties up, her slip and her skirt down, tugging up her stockings. The shawl that was roped around her neck—she undid the knot, straightening the shawl—she had made it with her own hands—and put it over her head, wrapping the ends of it around her neck and back across her shoulders. Her gloves—she took them from her pocket. "Is there anything like toilet paper in that stuff you found?"

"There is toilet paper," he answered. She turned her head, looking back to him. She had used the only tissue she had that last time. He was digging through a

36

knapsack, then reached something out—it was olive-drab. He said, "Here, catch," and threw it—she caught it fumblingly, basketing it as it fell into her lap. She put it in her coat pocket and started to try to get up again, her legs stiff, wobbly—she tried to remember the last time she had eaten. She stepped down, almost falling, into the snow. She heard Blackburn calling after her over the howl of the wind, "Remember—don't get lost. Because I won't come looking for you."

She was starting to cry, sagging against the fuselage of the Russian helicopter. She thought of Paul Ruben-stein—she loved Paul so hard. She thought of Mi-chael—and of Madison, who had become like a sister to her, sharing secrets, hopes. She thought of her mother, Sarah Rourke. Of her father, John Rourke.

And she thought of Natalia—Natalia who had saved her own life by letting a man get very close to entering her, making him think that somehow she could no longer resist him, then taking his knife and killing him.

Annie started to walk, squinting her eyes against the snow, pulling the shawl up to cover her mouth and nose, protect her face from the needles of ice as much as possible. She tried to tell herself that perhaps Natalia had told her the story once—but Natalia hadn't, Annie knew inside herself. It was the Sleep—it had somehow expanded something in her.

Through her squinted eyes, snow already encrusting her lashes, she could see a hummock of snow, perhaps rock beneath it, and she leaned into the wind, fighting her way toward it.

She would urinate. She would return—like a good girl—to the helicopter, fix Blackburn his food, force herself to eat. Despite hunger, she had no taste to eat. She would survive. And this night—even if it meant her eventual death, she would kill Blackburn before she would let him take her.

37

It was very cold as she passed to the other side of the rock, squinting her eyes against the tears and ice, beginning to hitch up her clothes . . .

They sat in the helicopter, eating from the rations they had brought, John Rourke listening as the others spoke. "The radiator hose just went. I replaced the hose and we melted snow and gradually refilled the radiator, mixing it with the antifreeze you had stored in the toolbox in the back of the truck."

Sarah clapped Paul on the thigh. "Well, as John would say, it pays to plan ahead." And she looked past Paul into Rourke's eyes. "What else do you have in that truck?"

Rourke let himself smile. "You might be surprised."

"Father Rourke — when we found where the helicopter had landed — we thought—"

John Rourke folded his arms about his de facto daughter-in-law's shoulders. "Madison — you're very sweet." She rested her head against his left shoulder.

Michael spoke. "We have to get Annie back. I'm well enough to travel — I saw that look in your eyes, Dad. I mean, it's not as if I'll be walking."

Rourke nodded. "I've been thinking about this. Wherever Karamatsov and his armies and his machines come from, wherever his machines were built—"

"The Underground City," Natalia supplied. "The dying boy on the battlefield."

Rourke nodded slowly, "Blackburn is the Soviet agent. That's where he's gone. There's no other reason why he'd fly north rather than south to link up with Karamatsov's forces. That must have been part of Blackburn's deal. When the Eden Project shuttles returned, he had a place to go. Only a fool or a patriot would have done what he did, infiltrating the Eden

Project, risk his life, give up his present life—only a fool or a patriot would have done that without an escape clause."

"I don't think he's either," Natalia murmured.

"Neither do I." Rourke nodded. "So he's got a destination, and evidently took Annie as insurance in case we caught up with him before he reached his destination. And . . ."

"Say it," Paul said slowly. "He took her—because after five hundred years, just in case—in case—"

"Because she's a woman," Elaine Halversen whispered. Kurinami, silent, eating slowly, nodded.

"Yes," Natalia nodded. "For that."

"If he touched her—I'll rip his fuckin' heart out," Paul said softly.

John Rourke only nodded, then, "With a helicopter, he's going to avoid crossing long expanses of water unless he has to. So it's evident what he's doing. Cross Canada to Greenland, then cross Greenland and make the hop to Iceland, then Scotland or Norway—pretty much equidistant. But I'd say Norway. More direct route to get him into the Soviet Union."

Natalia was opening and closing the Bali-Song, slowly, not with her usual blink-of-the-eye rapidity. "An underground city in the Urals."

"Yes," Rourke nodded.

"But how would we find it?" Kurinami asked through a mouthful of food. "We don't have any observation craft that can get high enough to search for variances in the infrared. . . ."

"Colonel Mann's people. His fighter plane's'll also outdistance these helicopters, Blackburn's or ours. Where's an SR-71 when you really need it" he said, shaking his head.

John Rourke stretched his legs, "But even though Mann's spread thin, he can get a few fighters up. He lost a third of his available forces in the battle for the Complex, lost a lot of his equipment and disabled men and equipment in the fight against Karamatsov. Between guarding the Complex, the small force he has following Karamatsov's retreat to pinpoint him, and the beefed-up security at Eden Base, we can't rely on him for much more than reconnaissance. But right now that's what we need." Rourke leaned forward, rubbing his hands together. "All right—here's what we'll do unless somebody's got a better idea. We've got plenty of fuel aboard both choppers. If I'm right that Blackburn's somewhere in Canada heading to Europe via Iceland, he'd probably be in Greenland by now, unless he stopped. He might stop in Greenland. But he's going to have to stop—six hundred miles or better to the nearest landfall once he leaves Iceland and he's the only pilot. He wouldn't try that on no sleep unless he's an idiot, and he's not. There's no guarantee he'll stop in Iceland, but I'm betting he will and right now that's the only option we've got. With the speed those two machines have, we can cover a reasonably thorough air search of Iceland—he can't hide the chopper and there'd be no way to effectively camouflage it. We should be able to see it miles away. Iceland, if my geography is correct, is about the size of the state of Georgia, maybe a little smaller. If there's snow this far south, Iceland should be covered with snow and ice. The helicopter's black. Should stick out like a sore thumb. The missile-targeting equipment aboard our gunships is heat-sensing—we can leave that running and possibly pick up a fire source, maybe even engine heat if we get near enough just after they land. If we miss them, Colonel Mann's fighter planes can be cutting a zigzag pattern northeast from La Havre— where it used to be—and out along the Norwegian coast up to the Barents Sea, then back. If we miss the chopper, the observation craft won't. All of us—we'll get her back."

Madison whispered, "With the help of God."

Rourke stood up, downing the rest of his coffee. "Let's secure the truck, get a position on it, and Colonel Mann can send someone for it. We're moving."

Chapter Four

Annie Rourke assumed the survival rations had been irradiated to prevent the natural process of desication resultant from the unavoidable bacteria, much as her father had planned ahead and irradiated the meat and other perishable foodstuffs in the freezers at the Retreat. At least she hoped the rations had been irradiated, as she heated the water over the small-camp stove. She had wrapped a blanket around her over her clothes, further insulation against the cold, the helicopter lashed down with ropes and stakes against the wind, Blackburn having constructed a lean-to which served now as a windbreak while she prepared the food.

The headache had not all been from the long delay in relieving her kidneys—but she assumed food would cure it, waiting for the water to boil. It took longer, her father had told her, than it used to in the days before the sky had caught fire and consumed not *all* life as they had once supposed, but most life. It took longer for water to boil, because the air was so much thinner now. And she supposed that at almost seventy degrees north latitude, the air was thinner still, but it seemed comfortably breathable, albeit frigid.

Her memory grasped at something she had either

read in a book once or heard spoken in one of the near-memorized videotaped movies her father kept at the Retreat—"A watched pot never boils." She looked away from the pot, lest the old saying be true. But then she suddenly realized that it couldn't be. Perhaps a watched teakettle—the kind that whistled—might never boil, but a pot, if never watched, would never be known to boil, might boil away all its contents. She looked back at the pot—the water was boiling.

Despite the circumstances, she found herself smiling.

And they were searching for her—somehow she knew that. They were searching for her now.

"How's it coming?" she heard Blackburn say over the howl of the wind. She knew he stood behind her, but she didn't turn to look at him. "How's it coming? I said."

"The water just started to boil—only take a few minutes now," and she began opening one of the foil-wrapped packages, seeing Blackburn at the corner of her peripheral vision, sitting on one of the two survival blankets. Annie knelt on the other one. If her father were in this position, or Natalia—either of them would have used the time profitably. "Where is this Underground City?"

"In the Ural Mountains. It was functional and wholly self-sufficient before what your people call the Night of the War. When the war came and then the Conflagration, it just went right on. It had to have—otherwise there wouldn't have been any Soviet helicopters, none of this advanced technology."

Annie Rourke laughed, looking at him for the first time since he had rejoined her. "A woman kneeling before a pot of boiling water in the middle of a snowstorm is advanced technology?"

Blackburn grinned. "You know what I mean," and

his voice dropped as she handed him one of the prepared meal packets — it looked like beef stroganoff of some sort, but the writing on the packets was Cyrillic and she read no Russian. "Look — ahh — you're a very pretty girl. I've been thinking, Annie. I don't want to frighten you. I really don't mean you any harm. I hadda get out with my life. You were my best insurance policy. And there's nowhere else I can leave you."

"Give me some rations — you won't need much — and a couple of extra blankets and a flare pistol — I'll take my chances. They'll be looking for me."

"No — I won't do that. I'm an American — not a Russian. I kinda like American girls. I don't know what kinda ugly servants of the state they've got at the Underground City. I like what I see."

She began eating her food, remembering — was it advice? — Natalia, softening her words into a question. "And what if I don't like what I see?"

"Is that how it is?"

"You kidnapped me. You treated me like some kind of animal."

"I can be kind, Annie — really kind. I really can."

Annie took a spoonful of her food — it was something like chicken and rice, but flat-tasting. She wondered if it was the company. "I don't know," she lied. "What choice do I have?"

"Not much, I'll admit," he smiled, taking some of his food.

She balanced the food packet against the box from which it had come, using her gloved left hand to pick up the boiling pot, pouring some of the still-hot water into the solitary cup. There was freeze-dried or dehydrated coffee or tea in it — she wasn't sure which since it smelled like neither. She stirred it with the handle of her spoon.

She extended her left hand to Blackburn—she offered him the cup. He took it, smiling . . .

The configuration of land and water below them matched the configuration of Hamilton Inlet, Quebec, on the five-century-old map in Rourke's hands. Rourke spoke into the headset microphone. "Akiro—here's where we part company. You follow the coast like we planned—until you reach Alpatok Island off Newfoundland—then take that adjusted compass heading we worked out. Over."

"Yes, John—between us—we shall find her! Kurinami over."

"Good luck—Rourke out," and Rourke set down the headset—he could hear if Kurinami tried reaching him, and Sarah and Paul would be taking turns monitoring the frequencies on the portable transmitter, trying to pinpoint a stray transmission from Blackburn or, if by some miracle Annie had overpowered him, an SOS from Annie.

It had been decided—Rourke had himself decided—that the most potentially efficacious course of action was for Kurinami, Elaine Halversen, Michael, and Madison to follow the route Blackburn almost certainly had to have taken, along the Canadian coastline and then to Greenland. It was a single-pilot mission.

But his was a two-pilot mission—Natalia and himself, to fly over water, making a straight-line course for Greenland, the helicopter's fuel tanks topped off, the distance to the next landfall something he didn't want to contemplate, but had calculated as accurately as map and compass would allow.

He banked to starboard, heading out to sea, in the distance to the north icebergs visible. His suspicion had been becoming slowly confirmed—that there had

45

been a major magnetic shift—compass readings the further north they had come becoming more and more erratic. But it would soon be night, and then the stars could serve as his navigational beacons, Natalia taking the controls, Rourke using his binoculars to scan the heavens. If the night were overcast, he would be shooting craps with their lives that he could handle the compass abnormalities.

Sarah came forward, kneeling between Rourke and Natalia, talking a little loudly over the whirring of the rotor blades, but it was the only way to be heard. "What if they didn't come this way, John? I mean— well—what if they didn't?"

"There's nowhere else he could be going, Sarah. If we can't intercept them, we'll find that Underground City—and we'll get inside somehow."

"Do you think he's—ahh—"

He looked at his wife. Natalia was turning to face her, touched her left hand lightly to Sarah's right shoulder. "Sarah—Annie is very smart—if anyone could avoid—well—could avoid that—I feel it—inside me I feel it."

John Rourke looked ahead—the whitecaps were building, and there would likely be a storm—he could see heavy gray patches of cloud that looked like harbingers of a front, far to the north of them, blocking their path. He hoped Natalia was right . . .

Annie felt almost overfull, her second meal of the day, but it was already night. No lean-to this time, but a tent, taken from survival stores already aboard the helicopter. And there had been a bottle of vodka—she wondered if it was for the medicinal needs of Soviet helicopter pilots.

Forrest Blackburn had taken a drink from the bottle,

46

passing it to Annie. She had taken a sip from the bottle, trying to make it appear as though she had taken more than a sip, hurriedly but not too hurriedly returning the bottle to Blackburn.

The flight over open water in daylight had terrified her, and when the night had come, she had studied the luminosity of the instruments, studied the silhouette of the man who currently held her life in his hands. And now she studied his face in the light of the Soviet counterpart of a Coleman lantern. He sipped again at the vodka.

The moment was coming—it was inevitable.

She had no idea what she would do, if she succeeded, other than go to the tied-down helicopter and try the radio, see if somehow she could contact help. If she could not, she would die here. But there were some things worse than death, she thought. Taking Blackburn to her breast would be such a thing.

He was staring at her—she tried to smile a little, without making the smile look too obvious or too false, or both. "You're going to get drunk," she told him.

"No—I won't get drunk. If I got drunk, I might pass out, then we'd both miss tonight."

Annie said nothing.

Blackburn spoke again. "You probably think I'll get drunk and you can kill me and slip out to the radio. Well—you can't." He reached into his coverall pocket, under his coat. "See this?"

It was a little flat piece of some type of fiberboard, with tiny wires set into it, the wires forming some sort of pattern. She guessed it was a circuit. "I see it."

"This runs the radio. No spare part—I checked." He closed his fist around the piece of fiberboard, crushing it in his hand.

"You're a fool, Forrest Blackburn," she whispered.

"No—more insurance, Annie Rourke," and he

smiled. "I had no one to talk to. I know the location of the Underground City. Don't need a radio to find it. And I sure don't want you getting to that radio and sending out a distress signal to your people." The wind howled around the tent, the tent vibrating with it, but keeping its integrity.

She leaned back, further, against the sleeping bag, letting the blanket drop from around her shoulders, her coat already open, pushing the shawl down from her hair.

"Is that an invitation?"

"I don't want to die. I don't have a choice. There's no sense getting beaten up and losing anyway. But—" and she told the truth now—"I've never done this. Never once. So you'll have to help me."

He stood up, his head almost touching the dome of the tent, his body wobbling a little as though he were about to lose his balance. But, if that was what it had been, he regained his balance, standing there, looking down at her. "You're a pretty girl, Annie—the hair, the eyes—I like long hair. I like brown eyes. You have any idea how good it is to see a girl in a dress with long hair and all, when all the other women you see are wearing the same kinda work clothes you're wearing, their hair almost as short as yours? When I took this job for Karamatsov—well, I never realized how it would be to wake up five hundred years in the future—everything gone. No friends. Nobody knew you. The Eden Project people—hell. All of 'em—dewy-eyed liberal idealists. But you—you're something different, Annie. I didn't think it'd be this easy. But I'm glad. I would have raped you—you know that?" She didn't think he wanted an answer. "But I didn't want it that way. I'll be good to you. You'll be safe with me."

Forrest Blackburn came around to her side of the lantern, dropped to his knees, his left hand touching at

48

her left leg just above her combat boot, his hand trailing along her stockinged calf, under the hem of her skirt, her slip, stopping when the fingers touched bare flesh. "You're soft—very soft to touch."

She realized suddenly that this man was trying to be nice, to be decent in his way, to make her feel comfortable, wanted—it sickened her that she was deceiving him, that she wanted nothing but to kill him. "You have a nice voice," she told him softly. "And your hands aren't cold." Both hands touched her left leg now, beneath her clothes. He withdrew his hands, unbuckling his pistol belt, putting it down beside the lantern. She looked away from the light. She could see the outline of the pistol butt silhouetted against the tent wall, that and the sheath for the bayonet. She looked back into his eyes, feeling Blackburn's breath—hot, smelling a little of the vodka—against her cheek, his lips touching at her forehead. She closed her eyes, feeling his lips touch at her left eyelid, linger there for an instant. She felt something as though somehow she was becoming moist—she shivered.

"What is it, Annie?"

"I'm cold," she whispered, and it was true in part.

He lay down beside her, his left hand beginning to explore beneath her sweater, pushing up along her blouse, in the gap between the buttons, his fingers touching the flesh of her abdomen. She closed her eyes tightly, folding her arms around his shoulders, inside herself whispering, "God forgive me—Paul, forgive me." She touched her lips against Blackburn's left cheek—his cheek was rough, unshaven, like her father's cheek sometimes when she would kiss him good morning as a little girl. She was feeling sick. His left hand found her right breast, pushing up the bra cup, his fingers touching gently at her right nipple. She moaned with the touch, Blackburn's lips crushing down on hers, making her respond—Was she responding to lead him on, to lull him into believing her? Or because he was exciting her? She didn't know—there was no time to think. Her left hand trailed down along Blackburn's right side—her fingers felt something. The butt of the pistol. The knife would be surer, but less instantly deadly. She had seen him check his pistol, and the chamber had been loaded. What if he hadn't kept it that way? His lips touched at her neck, his right hand knotted in her hair, pulling her head back—she could hardly breathe. His left hand was under her clothes now, not at her breast, but pulling down her panties—she could feel the coldness of the night air inside the tent, the roughness of his hand.

Her left hand found the flap of the holster—it was one of the M-12s, and she tugged down at the latch, freeing it. Her father had shown her this, all the weapons accessories he had, and all the weapons. She edged her left thumb against the lip of the fabric holster, Blackburn's fingers exploring her now—she felt pain and sucked in her breath, hearing the tiny scream as though somehow she were outside her own body, an observer. She could almost see him on top of her, see his face beside hers, see her bunched-up skirt and slip, his hand vanished beneath the clothes, working at her. Her body was trembling. She had the pistol free, settling her left hand around the butt—it felt as thick in the butt as Paul's High Power pistol. She had fired a pistol like this—her father had one in the armory at the Retreat.

She worked her left thumb against the safety, easing it upward, this time making herself moan as he touched her, to cover the click of the safety. She moved the pistol by feel, trying to see it in her mind. If she pressed it against his side to fire, would it still fire? Was it like a .45? She couldn't remember. But there was no other way. She sucked in her breath with a tiny scream — half voluntary, half involuntary — her thumb working back the hammer to full stand. She couldn't risk the long, double-action pull. She remembered now — with this pistol, there was a loaded chamber indicator. She moved her left thumb forward, along the slide, feeling for the loaded chamber indicator to protrude — it didn't.

His fingers were delving deeper into her now, her body moving under his, as though it had no will of its own anymore.

The knife — it had to be the knife. He had unloaded the chambered round.

The bayonet's grip — she felt it, closed her left fist over it. In her mind, she tried to see the sheath — a snap closure that ringed the handle. Her left thumb pried at it, and she moaned again to cover the noise. She started edging the knife out of the sheath, the pistol belt weighing it down, her body moving under his body. Her right hand — he was holding it now, bringing it to his crotch — she felt the hardness there, felt him draw her hand to the zipper at the crotch of his coveralls — she started tugging the zipper down, his hand returning to explore her, his lips against her neck. She sucked in her breath as the snap pieces made a scratching noise against the blade of the bayonet.

It was free. His zipper was down.

She closed her eyes tightly, reached inside his pants, and found his testicles, then closed her fist around them, her nails gouging into them as her left hand hammered toward him, down, into the center of his back, Blackburn screaming, "Bitch!" She pried the knife out as his right hand closed on her throat, her legs locking his left hand between them, her right hand twisting, ripping at his testicles now, her teeth biting into his cheek, the bayonet hammering down again,

51

into his right kidney, then out, down again, again into the kidney, then out, then down, into the spine, his body going rigid over her, his breath coming in a long hot rush against her face—there was a wetness in her hand and a smell like bleach.

Annie Rourke closed her eyes so she wouldn't see his dead eyes staring at her. It was as if Forrest Blackburn were asking, "Why?"

Chapter Five

She had washed the white liquid from her hand with the remainder of the warm water from the pot and the soap she had washed her hands with earlier before preparing the meal.

The knife was still in his back.

She would never remove it. There was a survival knife aboard the helicopter — she could take that.

The Beretta pistol — she had loaded the chamber but only after pushing the muzzle of the emptied pistol against the blanket and trying to pull the trigger — the slide had worked back and the trigger had jammed. If the pistol had been chamber-loaded and she had pressed it against Blackburn's side, if she had done it hard enough, it might not have discharged and he would have killed her.

It was cold as she knelt on the opposite side of the tent, on the opposite side of the lantern from him, but she had raised her skirt and slip, removed her sweater, opened her blouse, and, shivering, washed herself with the warm soapy water where he had touched her.

She would tell Paul, if she lived — tell him all of it. She wondered if he would forgive her, or if he would see anything that needed forgiving. She rinsed the soap away, toweling herself dry with an extra blanket, the rough wool even rougher feeling against her body. She dressed herself, winding the blanket around her—the wet corner would dry; the other blanket was under Blackburn's body. She left the tent, the howl of the wind tearing at her ears as she opened the flap—but she went behind the tent, did what she had to do, and used the last of the packet of toilet paper—she hoped there was more aboard the helicopter. Her left hand had never released the pistol since the moment she had left the tent, and as she entered the tent again, reflexively she aimed the pistol at Blackburn—but he could not have been more dead. His sphincters—if that was what they were called—had relaxed, and there was a horrible smell in the tent now. But she forced herself to search his pockets. A Swiss Army knife—all of the Eden Project crew carried them. A handkerchief. She left the handkerchief and took the knife.

She caught up one of the survival blankets, wrapping this over the woolen blanket already around her. She would need to make leg warmers and foot coverings for herself—the combat boots wouldn't do to keep her feet from frostbite. And the wind blew beneath her skirt. She took the other blanket, then stuffed the pockets of her coat with packets of the survival rations Blackburn had retrieved.

The helicopter—perhaps he had lied about the radio. But where had he gotten the printed circuit?

She left the tent again, swathed in the blankets, her shawl, her coat, hugging the blankets tight around her legs. The helicopter—she wedged her body against the wind and the driven ice spicules toward it, no real reason to go to the machine except for the survival knife—she could not fly the machine.

Annie Rourke reached the helicopter, clamboring aboard as she wrenched the fuselage door open, into the cockpit, closing the door, securing it locked—she didn't know why. It was like she imagined a tomb would be.

The night had been something that had not come, but instead been something they had flown into, a dull orb of sun on the horizon, seeming just to be there and then gone, as though it had never been.

She activated the electrical systems, having learned that much watching Blackburn. She found the radio — she would not talk into it, lest the Russians be monitoring the frequency. To be saved by them would be no salvation at all.

But the radio made no sound.

There was a red button beneath it, the button protected by a wire-cage cover which she removed. She depressed the red button, the button lighting. Depressing it again did not turn it off. "Shit," she hissed.

She killed the electrical system, taking the flashlight off the dashboard and turning it on — the beam was weak, because of the extreme cold, she assumed. She started aft, to explore what might be useful to her survival. More emergency rations, these newer-looking, less artfully packaged. The survival knife — not much of a knife, really, but sturdy enough, a synthetic-seeming leather-washered handle, a solid butt cap that could be used for hammering, the blade six inches, roughly Bowie-shaped with sawteeth on the spine. It was stainless steel, or something like it. The sheath was a synthetic that looked like leather but not quite — and it seemed brittle in the cold. She pocketed it with the survival food and continued her search. A lensatic compass — the needle spun and settled, but bobbed continuously at least ten degrees. "Terrific," she told herself. A small pouch — fishing gear. She recognized fishing gear, had seen it, had had her father show her how it worked. But there were no fish — then again, perhaps the Soviets knew something she did not. She took the kit and set it aside. An emergency medical kit, even to the red cross symbol against the white background. She inspected the contents quickly. There were several sutures and she could use these with the fishing line to fashion the blankets into woolen trousers to protect her legs. It would also be something to do, to keep her mind off the inevitability of death, she realized.

A flare gun and flares to go with it. These might be useful — maybe.

No weapons. The machine guns aboard the helicopter could perhaps be dismounted, but not carried conveniently. Blackburn's U.S. pistol and the Soviet survival knife and the M-16s would do well enough as weapons.

The tent was the logical place to stay the night — or however long she stayed. Blackburn's body — she could drag it out on the blanket and — Annie lowered her face into her gloved hands, balling her hands into fists, knotting her fists against her eyes. She wept . . .

She could not sleep, and her hands trembled — with the cold and with fear — as she used the suture and the fishing line to stitch together the pants that she had cut out using the survival knife. What remained of the blanket she would use to fabricate belt loops and a belt to tie them about her waist since there was no elastic, no zipper (except the ones on Blackburn's coveralls). She judged there would be enough of the fishing line to meet her sewing needs. She had found a rope in the helicopter, but was not prepared to cut any of it as a belt for the blanket pants — she had no idea of the terrain, and an extra two feet of rope might have more vital uses than as a belt.

She was stitching along the inside seam of the right leg when she heard the sound.

The wind, she told herself, squinting in the lamplight over her sewing.

56

She heard the sound again, loosing the sewing, with her left hand, the needle slipped into the fabric to prevent its loss. She let go of the pants, letting them fall onto her lap, drawing both her hands under her blankets, waiting there, listening. She had adjusted Blackburn's pistol belt to her waist and wore it snugged around the outside of her coat. She had thrown away the bayonet sheath, replacing it with the fake leather survival knife sheath and the knife itself. But her right hand reached to the holster, opening the flap, drawing out the Beretta 92-F, slipping it from beneath the blankets.

If her brother, or Paul, or her father had found her, none of them—even Michael with his sometimes-bizarre sense of humor—would have prowled around the tent. Blackburn's body had seemingly been heavier to haul in death than to support over hers in life, and she had dragged him only a short distance from the tent, covering his body with the folded-over blanket, leaving the drifting snow to do the rest.

She heard the sound again—saw the tent wall beside her move inward, as if buckling, then the impression of whatever had bumped against it was gone. Her hands shook, both holding the Beretta. "Who's out there!" She screamed the words.

She had read stories of ghosts—Blackburn. Had he come back from the dead?

Annie Rourke told herself that was impossible.

She set the pistol in her lap, pulling on her gloves, making a mental note to fashion sack-like mittens from remnants of the blanket material, to further protect her hands.

Gloves on, she took the Beretta in her tiny right fist, working the safety off, pushing her sewing aside with her left hand, gathering her blankets around her as she stood. "Who is—" She didn't finish it—movement against the wall of the tent again.

No one could live here. She would have heard the sound of a helicopter landing.

It was the wind—the wind had made the tent buckle inward—a strong gust, very strong. But why only in one spot? she asked herself.

It happened again—she stabbed the Beretta toward it, almost firing. But a bullet hole in the tent wouldn't be easily patched, and the wind would rip it larger.

"I've got a gun—if you've seen the body outside, you know I'm not afraid to kill. Who are you?" She kept her voice even, loud enough to be heard, she thought, outside the tent. Perhaps Russians—and they didn't speak English?

She walked forward, hugging the blankets around her with her left hand, clutching them at her breasts, her right fist balled on the pistol.

She stopped at the tent flap. "Go away!"

The sound again—like a howl, but not; like shouted words of anger, but not human.

Blackburn—she shivered.

Annie Rourke opened the tent flap, the wind assailing her, whipping at her skirt, at the blankets that cocooned her.

The storm had intensified, and she could see nothing in the darkness. The flashlight—it was where she had left her sewing.

She heard the sound again.

She fired the pistol once into the air. "Whoever the hell you are—I mean it!"

The moaning sound.

She told herself it couldn't be Forrest Blackburn because Forrest Blackburn was dead—she had seen enough of death to know it when she saw it.

She worked the safety down, then back up, to drop the hammer but make the pistol ready for a quick double-action shot.

Annie Rourke stepped away from the tent—in the darkness, there would still be the glow through the canvas or whatever it was—she would be able to find it again. Unless the lamp went out. . . . She worked all the possibilities in her head, trying to do like her father always did, would do now, trying to plan it all ahead.

She heard the sound, and turned toward it—it came from the direction in which she had dragged Forrest Blackburn's body.

"There's no such thing as a ghost!" she screamed, stabbing the pistol toward the darkness.

The moaning sound—she fired the pistol toward it. The sound stopped—she worked the safety again to drop the hammer, then worked it up to the fire position.

It was the main problem with being a girl, she had always thought—your voice wasn't deep enough to be taken seriously and you went out of your way to make yourself look gentle, and so how did you look tough?

She advanced, slowly, the blankets still clutched at her breasts in her left fist, the pistol close to her body like her father had always taught her.

It wouldn't be long until she reached the spot where Blackburn's body lay—she had to see it, and in the seconds since leaving the tent her eyes had become accustomed enough to the swirling darkness that she could see.

Something came against her body and she fell forward, no time to turn the pistol, to fire, and her head impacted against Forrest Blackburn's face and she saw the dead eyes looking at her. But she had summoned the courage to close the eyelids, to shut them. Why were they open? She screamed, rolling onto her back. Something huge hulked over her.

She had seen pictures of bears—the thing seemed

incredibly huge. But bears were dead. Forrest Blackburn was dead. She stabbed the pistol toward the apparition, toward the shape, making to fire, but her right hand suddenly went numb and the pistol flew from her grasp.

And the thing started to reach for her and she pushed to her feet and started running into the blackness . . .

He had taken sightings on Polaris, juxtaposing these against the accuracy of his Rolex, to get a fix on latitude and longitude, just before they had passed into the cloud bank—the compass seemed to be holding to a steady degree of error and Rourke compensated for it as he plotted their position in the map light, the machine bouncing, lurching in the churning air around them. Natalia, in the copilot's seat, spoke. "I'm taking her down—we can use the running lights to make sure we avoid the whitecaps—the storm at this altitude will tear us apart."

Paul Rubenstein crouched between them. Sarah at the radio, listening for a distress call, whispered, "She's out in this, maybe—shit—"

"If Blackburn doesn't know how to survive in extreme cold, Annie does. I taught her, just like I taught Michael. Blackburn's no dummy—if he doesn't know what to do and it sounds like Annie does, he'll listen to her. If they're on the ground. And if they were on the ground before this started and they're in the same weather system we are, they won't go airborne. This could pull it out of the fire for us, Paul."

"If we live that long," Natalia added cheerlessly.

Rourke just looked at her and smiled, knowing she couldn't see him—her eyes were riveted ahead. He felt the queasy feeling in his stomach as the helicopter lurched, Natalia announcing, "I'm taking her down."

"All right—let me know when you want me to spell you."

"No hurry—I rode one of those bucking bulls once in a bar. I was on an assignment with Yuri—you never met him. Well, you did—after those brigands killed him, right before you and Paul found me wandering in the desert. Yuri played the redneck—always. He wore cowboy hats and boots and snap-front cowboy shirts and spoke English with a perfect Southern accent. But it's like this, flying this helicopter—like riding the bull. You just have to hang on and watch out that it follows a pattern."

"Did you make it?" Paul asked. "I mean—did you stay on until the bull stopped?"

She didn't flicker her eyes from the windshield—rain and balls of ice and sleet lashed it—"How about I tell you after the storm subsides, Paul!" she smiled.

Behind him, John Rourke heard Sarah shout. "A radio signal—it sounds like it's Russian. I don't know. But I hear it—in and out—just repeating."

"What frequency?" Rourke snapped, turning in his seat, staring toward her in the center of the fuselage.

"It's crossing frequencies—try between 121.500 and 121.600 megahertz."

Rourke twisted back in his seat, taking up his headphone set, working the dials for the radio, off the frequency shared with Kurinami's chopper and the fighter planes of Wolfgang Mann, tuning, the static becoming lighter as they dropped altitude, his eyes scanning the altimeter.

He heard it—it was the most simple of distress signals, and obviously a recording. The word was *Pahmageeyeh*—help.

Rourke cut out, shouting to Sarah, "Keep monitoring, Sarah," and then dialing into the frequency with

Kurinami. "Akiro—this is Rourke. Over. Akiro—come in—this is Rourke. Over." Nothing. He said to Paul, to Sarah, to Natalia, "If I can raise Kurinami and he can pick up the distress signal, we can work a triangulation, nail down the position." Into the headset, Rourke said again, "Kurinami—this is Rourke—do you read me? Over."

John Rourke prayed.

Chapter Six

The storm had subsided.

The triangulation had been made.

The tent and the Soviet helicopter had been sighted on an ice field.

Rourke's helicopter had landed.

The Soviet helicopter had been empty of life.

The tent had been partially blown down in the wind.

The body of Forrest Blackburn had been uncovered, buried several inches under the snow except for a rigored left arm which had extended ominously upward, as if a warning beacon — but a warning for what? Paul Rubenstein had wondered.

Sarah, John, Natalia — they had been with him as he had entered the tent, Sarah dropping to her knees beside pieces of blanket material, raising them toward her face. "Annie — she was sewing these."

"Wandered off, maybe," Rourke said slowly. "Natalia — let's get —"

But Natalia had left the tent.

Paul Rubenstein stepped out into the gray light, John Rourke beside him, Sarah after them as Paul looked back. Natalia was near the body of Blackburn, kneeling there. "Did you look closely at the body, John?"

"No — not yet."

"Several things—they tell a story, Paul—look around the body—Sarah—would you help him? Make a search area, say ten yards out, cover it, then expand it another ten yards. If that hole was a standard field survival cache—"

"What hole?" Paul asked her.

"The one you and Michael and Madison discovered. There were two M-16s in the tent. But there was no pistol. There should have been a pistol. Find it—if you can't, we'll know Annie has it."

"All right," Paul answered, but then, "What's peculiar about the body?"

John Rourke knelt in the snow beside Natalia. He answered Paul. "Multiple stab wounds—something the size of an M-16 bayonet or a Gerber—"

"Wait—"

John Rourke was helping Natalia roll over the body now, Paul drawing closer. Natalia said it. "Bayonet." An M-16 bayonet was buried up to the hilt in Blackburn's back where the spine would be. And the multiple stab wounds were evident. "Help me roll him over again, John," she said.

Paul started looking—for the pistol, he guessed, or whatever else might provide some clue.

Sarah, far to Paul's left shoulder, shouted, "I found it—over here." Paul ran toward her, John and Natalia coming as well now, Sarah holding what looked like a black semiautomatic in her right hand, brushing snow from it. "Safety's off."

John Rourke took the pistol from her—it was a Beretta 92SB-F, the fifteen-plus-one shot 9mm parabellum adopted by the U.S. military just prior to The Night of The War—John Rourke had one at the Retreat. Rourke was examining it. "One shot fired, maybe two, depending on whether there was one in the chamber to start with plus a full magazine or not.

These are good shooters—and Annie's a good shot. If she had a target she could see—and with visibility last night that could be questionable—she would have hit it. It couldn't have been some large force or she would have taken one or both of the M-16s."

"You—ahh—think she just wandered off? But she wouldn't—not without her gun, some weapon."

Natalia had disappeared again, and Paul heard her calling to them across the ice field. "I found something else." Paul broke into a run, toward her, John and Sarah flanking him, the sky a little brighter now but not much—he gathered it was as bright as it would get. Natalia had Blackburn's coverall's open, her gloved hands exploring his crotch. "He had recently ejaculated, but these stains in his underpants would indicate—well—that he didn't do it in someone." Paul swallowed hard. "He had scratch marks—as if something gouged at his testicles—a woman's nails, I'd say. He was making love to Annie, forcing himself on her, perhaps raping her or perhaps Annie had the good sense to make it appear she wanted him, or at least wouldn't resist. He was stabbed by Annie's left hand, assuming a missionary position on his part, so her right hand would have done—this," and she nodded toward Blackburn's open clothing. "Evidently, the act took place in the tent—since Blackburn is still wearing a coat and the knife is still in his back, but the coat is open. Annie had to have survived, to drag the body out—she probably used this blanket."

Rourke spoke—Paul Rubenstein felt he was listening to a conversation at 221 B Baker Street, the way Natalia was reconstructing the act, the look on John's face. "He was right-handed, if I recall correctly."

"Yeah—he was," Paul supplied.

"All right—so for Annie to get to the bayonet, which would have been carried on his left side most probably, he had removed the pistol belt or whatever he carried it on."

"The standard survival cache included emergency rations, emergency medical supplies, emergency fuel, an assault rifle of the native country, spare magazines and ammo, the sidearm of the native country, and the corresponding web gear necessary for transporting the sidearm comfortably. Also, the bayonet to accompany the rifle. Since there were two rifles, and considering the purposes of the survival cache, I would imagine this one was substantially more elaborate. Likely we'll find considerable fuel supplies aboard the helicopter."

"I'll have another look," Sarah volunteered.

"Sarah," Natalia called after her, "see what's in the pilot survival kit—inventory it and I should be able to give you an idea what Annie might have taken from it, then we can inventory what remains in the tent and at least determine what gear Annie has on her."

"All right," Sarah called back, running toward the helicopter.

Rourke, visibly shivering with the cold, said, "We'll need to break out the cold-weather gear. I can take the German machine airborne. Natalia—you and Paul fool with the Russian helicopter—see if you can get her airborne. I don't think there should be any problems." And John Rourke turned to Paul. "You take the radio set from the German helicopter—you and Sarah re-erect the tent as a shelter, and keep monitoring the radio for Natalia's machine and mine—we'll get on the same frequency. In the event we miss Annie from the air and she returns to the tent, you and Sarah'll be here."

"She couldn't have survived out there, could she?"

"She's never had to do it, but I taught her the principles of building an igloo-like structure for protection—if she had a knife, she could have done it. She was dressed reasonably warmly — if she erected a wind-break wall first, then built the rest of the structure — shit, I don't know," and John Rourke clasped Paul's shoulder.

Chapter Seven

A hunch was a curious thing, but Natalia Anastasia Tiemerovna had long ago determined that hunches — or, for members of her sex, what was called women's intuition — could sometimes prove out. Her hunch this time was really more what she considered an educated guess — that if Annie had left the tent and the helicopter and gone into the night across the ice field, she would have done so in panic or in fear. Being a Rourke, it was hard to imagine Annie so totally seized with panic as to do something irrational. But fear could grip anyone and send them running toward an unknown and potentially deadly fate in an attempt to escape the known and definitely deadly thing that was immediate. Natalia had no reason to support a hypothesis that Annie had done so, had run into the subarctic night to escape some terror. The hunch, or women's intuition, was simply judgmental as to where Annie would have gone.

The Soviet helicopter that she now flew alone over the ice field had landed at roughly just north of sixty-three degrees north latitude and almost dead on twenty degrees west longitude, just beneath what had been the Arctic Circle; had there been the polar shift that the compass variations strongly suggested, she could now be inside the Arctic Circle — the ice here suggested as much. There were mountains to the east of the position where the tent had been staked, and if she—Natalia— had been fleeing for her life, these mountains were where she would have gone. They would not have been visible in darkness, but had Annie survived the night, they would have been visible from anywhere on the ice field—a goal to aim for if the tent were somehow considered too dangerous. Blankets that should have been in the helicopter, according to the dictates of logic, were not in the helicopter. The survival knife that should have been in the helicopter was missing as well.

As she flew over the ice field now, she scanned the whiteness against the gray of the overcast sky for some sign of Annie or some sign of a survival shelter, but Natalia's goal was the mountains. As she flew a zigzagging search pattern, she could hear radio chatter between John and Sarah, John flying due north beyond what seemed to have at one time been a river course. John would reach his most northerly point, then head southwest, Natalia to turn roughly southwest as well, following the mountains toward the sea, both of them linking at the tent where Sarah and Paul monitored the radio and waited for the possible return of Annie.

John had expressed concern to her—Natalia—that the rescue signal, which John Rourke had shut off by smashing the device, would perhaps summon Soviet gunships from Europe. The once disabled radio which Natalia now monitored, had been jury-rigged into working order by scavenging parts from the intra-ship communications systems of both helicopters.

Beneath Natalia now was a physical feature she recognized, though her knowledge of Iceland was quite limited. It was Mt. Hekla, a massive volcano. Iceland was one of the most volcanically active regions on the face of the earth, geysers having passed below her regularly, their rivulets of steam rising into the frigid air, since the chopper had first gone airborne.

She cut in on the radio transmission. "John — this is Natalia. I'm not seeing anything. I'm heading up into the mountains as far as Annie might possibly have gotten — but the storm and the high winds . . . The snow doesn't seem touched below me. She may not have crossed here. Over."

"Same here, Natalia — no sign — no sign at all. We've gotta keep looking. Rourke out."

Natalia wanted to blink her eyes — but she was afraid that somehow in doing so she might miss the precious object of her search. Instead, she stared beneath her, through the chin bubble, hoping.

Chapter Eight

She had seen a bear in the zoo when she was a little girl. But she couldn't remember which zoo — the one in Atlanta or the one in Columbia, South Carolina? She opened her eyes. There was someone talking — to her? — but the language sounded oddly old and like no language she had ever heard, but in some ways like English.

It was the bear from — last night?

The bear turned toward her and it was a man, not a bear at all.

"What?"

The single word triggered, or seemed to trigger, an outpouring of words, but the words were no more intelligible than they had been before she had opened her eyes.

There was a dog — a real, living dog, the kind she remembered, only bigger, furrier, more like the wolves she had seen somewhere in reality and in some of her father's videotapes.

The man stood up — he was beside a fire, the fire sweet-smelling, but no wood present, just little brick-like things, four of them, the flame leaping from the point where the four brick-like objects touched at the center. They formed a small X-shape, or cross.

The dog stood up, but didn't move toward her, only

staring at her as though wondering what she was.

Annie looked around her—a cave of some sort, ice encrusting the walls, moisture condensing over the ice that lined the roof of the cave, some of the moisture dripping down like drizzling, icy rain, little stalactites of ice and water forming over her head.

The man walked closer to her. He was huge, the biggest human being she had ever seen, his reddish hair long and covering his ears, blending into his longish red beard, the red of the beard less bright than the red of the hair, the beard coming up high to his cheekbones, his eyes—blue, piercing—staring at her over the beard. He was dressed in leather and some type of cloth; the boots he wore, nearly to his knees, seemingly of leather; baggy, cloth trousers, green in color, stuffed into the tops of the boots. A leather shift from his shoulders to his knees, the hem of it reaching almost to his boottops, like a dress might. The leather shift was sleeveless, a round neck split at the front, open almost to his abdomen; beneath the leather shift, visible over his chest—massive, barrel-like—a green shirt of some heavy material, the shirt laced at the front like cowboy shirts she had seen in movies. The sleeves of the shirt were billowing, coming to the wrists with long, three-button cuffs.

His hands—he stuffed them into slash pockets in the sides of the black leather shift—were massive.

He smiled at her.

The dog barked—and she thought she was going to die but instead she only screamed.

The giant only laughed, shaking his head, returning to the fire.

Annie lay there, realizing that over the blankets that were still wrapped around her was a heavy, quilted thing—a sleeping bag, but opened flat. There was another one beneath her.

She watched the man—he was using a ladle to put some sort of liquid taken from the pot over the miraculously burning bricks into a cup. He put the ladle back in the pot, then gestured toward her with a cup.

Annie made herself smile. "Who are you?"

The man shrugged his shoulders, his face somehow looking apologetic. He said nothing, but still extended the cup of steaming liquid to her.

She was cold—she had to go to the bathroom, but that would wait—it would have to.

She sat up, the blankets falling from her shoulders, instantly colder. She rearranged them about her, the man standing, coming closer to her with the cup. She reached up to him, taking it, saying, "Thank you."

The man nodded as if understanding—not the words, but the intent of them. She held the mug in both hands, keeping her shoulders hunched up, rigid, to keep from losing the blankets. Annie blew across the surface of the cup to cool it, smelling it—like cinnamon, she thought. She sipped at it—she guessed there might be alcohol in it, but it tasted good and warmed her insides, the sweet smell not present in the taste, the taste indefinable but good. "What is this?"

She raised her eyebrows, raised her voice, tried to make it sound, look like a question.

The man nodded, smiling, saying something she couldn't have repeated to save her life, but it still tasted good.

The dog eyed her, not growling—she didn't really remember how to act around dogs.

She nodded, pointing to herself, freeing one of her gloved hands from the warmth of the cup. "Annie Rourke." She pointed to him. He nodded. "Annie Rourke," she said, pointing to herself again.

The man stabbed his massive right thumb at his

chest, saying slowly, "Bjorn Rolvaag."

She pointed to herself, saying, "Annie," and then to him, saying "Bjorn."

He said, "Annie," pointing to her, then to himself, "Bjorn," and then pointed to the dog, saying "Hrothgar."

She pointed to the dog. "Hrothgar?"

"Ja," the man nodded. "Hrothgar."

"Like Beowulf — Hrothgar in *Beowulf*," she nodded, the man's face showing he didn't understand.

"Where am I?"

He answered, "Lydveldid Island."

She gestured around her. "Where?"

And he pointed outside the cave, saying only one word. "Hekla."

"Hekla," she repeated. She sipped at the drink, watching the dog watch her, the leather-clad, red-haired and bearded green giant drinking from the ladle, water still dripping from the roof of the cave.

Chapter Nine

The helicopter search had availed them naught. Rourke had dismantled the tent, fabricating improvised snowshoes using the tent poles cut with a hacksaw from the German helicopter's toolkit, having bent the pole sections with great difficulty by hand, Paul helping him. Kurinami's helicopter was still several hours away, Sarah briefing Kurinami while Paul and John Rourke bent more of the tent pole sections. Natalia had already begun lacing the guy lines for the tent into a webbing to support the feet, Sarah, as she spoke, taking the slings from the two spare M-16s found in the tent and cutting them. The buckles that secured the slings and segments of the slings themselves would serve as foot bindings for the snowshoes.

Kurinami, Michael, Madison, and Elaine Halversen would swing north, looking for any signs of Annie—recent communication between Kurinami and Colonel Mann's fighter aircraft had yielded no word of unidentified Soviet helicopters or other aircraft crossing over the European continent from the direction of Greenland, and their support craft for refueling were themselves running out of fuel and would return to North America where Mann was ferrying in more fuel and more equipment almost hourly. A relay patched through between the fighters and Dr. Munchen, the de facto field commander for the Germans at Eden Base, indicated that Karamatsov's forces were segmented, the bulk of his force returning to the area of West Texas, more forces flying by way of North Africa to the West Texas staging area, the forces avoiding crossing over Georgia where Eden Base was located. Commander Dodd, overall commander of Eden Base, was aiding Munchen in digging in for battle. The space shuttles could not be moved any great distance and the information in their computer banks was too valuable to sacrifice by abandonment. Mann was planning on deploying a small force into Iceland within thirty-six hours at the outside to assist in the search for Annie.

Sarah conveyed all the information, rejoining Paul, Natalia, and John Rourke. She busied her hands, using a heavy needle of the type used to sew leather or canvas and a heavy thimble to attach the binding sections to the first completed pair of snowshoes, but her mind wasn't thinking of the task in her hands at all, but rather of her daughter. And of the man Annie wanted to marry. She looked across her work at Paul Rubenstein, working side by side with her husband, John Rourke. John had packed cold-weather gear in both pickup trucks when they had left the Retreat — all of them wore it now. He had secured cold-weather gear for Akiro Kurinami and Dr. Elaine Halversen from the Germans, the German gear lighter, more modern-seeming, but Sarah comfortably warm in the winter clothing her husband had provided. Once again, John Rourke had planned ahead. It was sometimes disgusting, sometimes comforting, that he did so, disgusting in that he was always right, comforting in that his forethought had saved their lives uncounted times.

With the hoods of their black parkas in place, the added bulk of the parkas, the snow pants, their mouths and noses swathed by the knit headgear worn beneath the hoods, John and Paul looked almost alike—except for John's greater height and the sunglasses he had always worn ever since Sarah had first met him—how many years ago! She had been doing volunteer nursing, and John had been interning for the medical career he never undertook. When they had met again, years later, little had changed in him. His face was leaner than it had been, his musculature better defined, and when he removed the glasses that masked his brown eyes, a look of sorrow she had seen only the vaguest hint of when they had earlier known one another.

Years in the CIA as a counterterrorist, a "case officer" as the euphemism went, and taking lives rather than saving them. As the years progressed after their marriage, he had become increasingly interested in survivalism, planning for some ultimate nightmare, yet all the while hoping, she finally had realized, that it never occurred, that his plans were for naught. There had been something that last time in Central America, when the reports had come in that he was missing and presumed dead and no one had told her anything else, and she had kept the children close to her and told herself that John Thomas Rourke was unkillable. And he had returned, his body covered with cuts and superficial wounds, bruises, a gunshot wound in his left leg, a knife wound. When he left the CIA, saying only that he had been set up and betrayed, she had thought his obsession with weapons, survivalism, all of it, would abate, that he would begin the practice of medicine—more than one doctor had told her that first time she had known John that he had gifted hands, hands and a mind quick enough to use them that most surgeons would have envied. But he had not.

Rather than medicine, he had chosen to write and teach—about weapons training, wilderness survival, spent every spare dollar and every spare hour building the Retreat. And more so than during the years he had spent in the CIA, she had felt them drawing apart.

But he had proven right. Whoever had first fired a missile or dispatched a bomber past the fail-safe point—if it would ever be known; she did not know it now—had started the global thermonuclear war between the United States and the Soviet Union. John had been away—he usually had been. She had taken her young children from the farm, their house destroyed after the gunfight and the gas explosion, determined to find John, while John had crashed a jet airliner in New Mexico, and began his cross-country trek with Paul Rubenstein, searching for her. It was during that time that John had met Natalia—but that he had known her before, Sarah was sure. And that time too was the time when John had fallen in love with Natalia, and Natalia with him, and for once, John Rourke had not "planned ahead."

He had found her, but there had been no end to the nightmare that had begun following The Night of The War. John had explained it and she still did not really understand it—but during The Night of The War, particulate matter had begun accumulating in the atmosphere, the particles electrically charged, and when heated, agitated. The charge had been building—the cause of the wild electrical storms and bizarre weather patterns that had begun after The Night of The War. Then one morning, the electrical charge had built to such a level that the sky became consumed with fire at dawn, the last dawn, and the flames followed the rising of the sun and scorched the entire planet, destroying all life.

But Sarah had survived—because John had planned ahead. With John, Natalia, Paul, her young son Michael, and her young daughter Annie, using stolen cryogenic chambers taken from the KGB, using cryogenic serum developed by NASA scientists for deep-space travel and without which the cryogenic chambers would have been perpetual living death, without which it would have been impossible to awaken. But when she awakened, John had already awakened, had awakened the children, spent five years with them teaching them all he could, then had returned to The Sleep while Michael and Annie grew, abandoned the childhood she had so cherished. She had awakened, in her mid-thirties, her children Michael and Annie respectively aged almost thirty and almost twenty-eight, her son off on some reckless adventure just like his father, her son returning with Madison, the survivor of another colony that had weathered the burning of the sky, but the twenty-fifth generation of these survivors. Pretty Madison — blonde, soft-spoken, gentle, feminine — and pregnant with Michael's child.

In her mid-thirties, Sarah Rourke would soon be a grandmother, her children her contemporaries — and all because of John and his having planned ahead. Annie was somewhere — Sarah looked across the ice field, her work with the snowshoe bindings finished — out there, and when Annie were found — Sarah told herself *when* was the word, not if — Annie would marry Paul Rubenstein. She smiled thinking of Paul — the supremely unlikely hero. An associate editor of a magazine from New York City, his father a retired Air Force colonel, like Paul's mother, dead five centuries ago. A Jew — she had never considered that she would have a Jewish son-in-law, but none of that really mattered. He was a good man, a gentle man, a fine man, heroic, loyal, quick. He had no heroic visage — his forehead was high, but from recession of hair, not high from nature's sculpture as was John's. His eyes were dark, but there was no hidden passion in them as

79

there always had been in John's brown eyes. He had a normal voice—neither high nor low, not the heroic, attention-demanding deep whisper of John Rourke. There was innocence in his face, decency—and he loved Annie very much, Annie falling in love with him as she had grown up in The Retreat, watching Paul in the cryogenic sleep.

Sarah Rourke considered her life. And she was pregnant—she was certain that in making love to John, she had let him do it. Had she wanted it? She still didn't know. A baby would recapture for her what John—she had at last grudgingly admitted in his wisdom—had taken from her. She could watch this baby grow up, be its mother, not its contemporary.

But she didn't want a baby as a device for holding a husband. His honor—his unrelenting honor. That he loved Natalia, perhaps more than he loved her, was obvious, but that he would not touch Natalia, would not abandon his wife, was obvious too.

There had always been this godlike perfection in John Rourke, and Sarah Rourke had found that living with such a man—was it impossible?

He was almost invariably clean-shaven, almost invariably controlled his temper, invariably was right, his decisions based on logic and the superimposed logic of genuine human decency. He was a knight-errant, a paladin, a demigod, a hero, comfortably wearing the perfect manhood other men strove for, pretended at. In his late thirties, he had the body of a twenty-five-year-old in perfect athletic trim, the few strands of gray in his thick, healthy-looking brown hair simply serving to heighten the innate dignity of his face. That he was a genius she had never doubted. Once, when it had been reported he was dead during that last mission in Latin America, she had begun to go through the copies of his personal papers, the originals of all important documents something he had immediately stored at The Retreat.

She had found medical and psychological profiles; how he had obtained them was something she had never asked. She knew enough of medicine to interpret the medical profiles. Strength, endurance, lung capacity, heart stress capacity—all above normal. The IQ—why it had been tested she did not know, but she imagined it had perhaps been in relation to his work in the CIA. She had blinked, not believing what she had seen, but then realizing more about her husband than she had ever known. Average for a young adult was one hundred plus chronological age. The one hundred forties were well into the genius level or on its very indefinite boundary, the one hundred sixties phenomenal. John Thomas Rourke—intelligence quotient one hundred eighty-six.

Her demigod—she watched him as he worked beside his best friend, Paul Rubenstein, and bent the last of the tent spars into its final shape for the last snowshoe.

John Thomas Rourke—she loved him.

Chapter Ten

Bjorn Rolvaag and the massive, furry dog at his heels, Hrothgar, navigated the rising ground decidedly more easily, she thought, than she could ever do it. "Hey—wait!"

Rolvaag turned toward her and she thought she saw him smile, but it wasn't easy to tell. He had covered his head and most of his face with something that looked like a ski mask, only looser, with individual holes for his eyes and a hole for his mouth, again the color of it green. She wondered if green were some sort of uniform here, or if perhaps he just liked the color because it did nice things with his red hair and beard and his blue eyes. He had apparently understood her intent, if not the words, and waited now, Hrothgar running in tight circles at his heels as Rolvaag leaned easily on his shoulder-height staff.

He had no rifle, no pistol that she had seen, but two edged weapons. Over the leather shift that came to his knees he wore a coat—green again—hooded and belted at the waist and coming to mid-calf length, but over the left breast a sewn-in sheath for a massive knife of some sort—she had not seen the blade shape, but from the pattern of the sheath, it seemed roughly Bowie-shaped. Belted over his coat, his left hand resting on its hilt now, was a sword, something like she had seen in movies, read of in Arthurian legends. Again, she had not seen the blade, but only the hilt and the sheath — but unless the sheath were overly large, the blade seemed wide and perhaps a yard in length.

Annie Rourke kept slogging after him, her stride not wide enough to fill his footsteps, but rather making a third footprint in the snow that covered the slope between each of his two. Over her blankets, she wore one of the sleeping-bag-like quilts wrapped over her head and as much around her body as she could and still be capable of walking normally. Her legs were cold above her stockings under her skirt, and the fabric of her slip against her thighs felt like thin ice.

She wanted to ask him how much further, and where, and what "further" was — but all of this was beyond the scope of their communications.

When she had nearly reached him, he began along the slope again, his staff in his right hand helping him to walk, his left gloved hand resting on the hilt of his sword as though walking here were the most casual of things to do, his massive backpack with the frame empty at the top and the second sleeping bag rolled at the bottom, unswaying on his back as he moved.

Hrothgar — whatever sort of dog he was — raced ahead, stopping, then racing back.

She gathered they were climbing Hekla, to which Rolvaag had alluded earlier, and Heckla was apparently a substantial mountain. Below them, in a valley, were geysers, steam rising from them, the steam seemingly captured in an artificial cloud layer that obscured the mountain slope some few hundred feet overhead. But the walk was more lateral now, she realized, noting that the steam cloud layer was getting no closer to them, Rolvaag picking his steps, shifting slightly up the slope and down, as though following some invisible path. She judged his height at about six-foot-six, his weight in excess of two hundred fifty pounds, but because of his size and, she imagined, because of the life he led, it seemed all muscle rather than excessive bulk.

The life he led—that he was alive at all was incomprehensible to her. And a dog?

She kept following him, the sleeping bag pulled so close around her face that sometimes it would slip over her eyes and she was unable to see. She would tug it away and continue, though the walk seemed never-ending. She wondered at times if it was—was he some sort of nomad without a base, a home? But the clothes—they were clean, the sleeping bag not possessed of any body-odor smell. The hair and the beard were immaculate, as though freshly washed and well-brushed or combed. His teeth, when he smiled, were perfect-seeming and white. His face, what was visible of the skin between the long hair and the magnificent mustache and beard, seemed not as skin would be for someone who constantly lived exposed to these temperature extremes. She had no way to judge accurately the ambient temperature but guessed that it was several dozen degrees below zero. Silently, she thanked God there was no wind to speak of. Her face where it was exposed already felt numb, her hands and feet numbing too. If the walk were of much greater duration, she would begin experiencing frostbite. Rolvaag, though, seemed literally unaffected by the cold.

The dog was sniffing—she remembered dogs only a little from childhood, but she knew what the dog had on his mind, watching with fascination because it was something that she had thought had ceased to exist. The dog urinated against a rock, then ran on a few steps, circling, raising its tail, circling, squatting, feces steaming in the snow as Annie walked up even with the dog, passing it, Rolvaag slowing down, to wait for his animal, she assumed.

The dog sprinted past her again, beyond Rolvaag, disappearing when the ground dipped suddenly, great clouds of steam rising from beyond the temporary horizon.

Rolvaag's pace quickened, Annie trying to do the same, her feet numb to the point of being difficult to raise them enough to walk. He ascended the rise, stopping, backlit as it were by the rising clouds of steam.

"Annie!" Rolvaag called. "Annie Rourke! Hekla!" And he gestured behind him, into the steam. She had thought they were climbing Hekla, and she now wanted to sink to her knees in the snow and ice and huddle against a rock outcropping, because if Hekla was still some distance away, whatever this mountain— she assumed it was that still—held for Rolvaag, she could not continue.

But Annie Rourke told herself that she had to, almost losing the sleeping bag that was around her as she used her hands to help her scale this newest summit, toward Rolvaag and the clouds of steam. He was extending his staff toward her and she reached for it, clasping it in her right hand, closing her fist around it, her fingertips without feeling now.

As she pulled herself up with the staff, Rolvaag reeling her in toward him with it, she noticed the staff for the first time in greater detail. It was made of some type of metal, its tip formed into a spike, and there were seams along the shaft, as though the shaft were joined in pieces. She wondered if it was hollow, used to secret objects part of Bjorn Rolvaag's gear?

She almost tripped, Rolvaag arresting her fall, catching her against him, laughing. She stared over the rise, toward the origin of the steam.

It was the first time in her life Annie Rourke had ever done it — she fainted.

Chapter Eleven

John Rourke shouldered his rifle—an M-16—muzzle down over his left shoulder, the Lowe Alpine System's Loco Pack on his back. He waved to the German helicopter—it was the better of the two machines and Natalia flew it, Sarah with her. Beside him, Paul Rubenstein said, "This should do some good—shouldn't it?"

"Is that a question or a statement?" Rourke asked, pulling his hood up over the black SAS Headover.

"A statement."

"Hmm," Rourke nodded, not agreeing, adjusting his dark-lensed aviator-style sunglasses as he spoke. "Well, Natalia seems to think that Annie would have headed this way. Since I don't have a better idea, I'm inclined to agree. With this black clothing we're wearing, and sticking to the compass course we prearranged, Natalia—or Kurinami, when he gets here—shouldn't have any trouble finding us. Searching from ground level seems to be the only alternative."

"You didn't say anything about when Mann's people get here," Paul observed.

"No—honestly speaking, if we haven't found her by then, considering the clothing she had, considering the terrain, the temperature—I don't think it would do any good. So what are we wasting time for?" John Rourke almost whispered. "But yeah—we'll keep looking until we find her, however—we—ahh—shit—come on," and Rourke started ahead.

The country they began to cross—long, angular valleys, high barren ridges, the white starker seeming against the grayness of the sky—would be navigable on foot unaided, but time was their enemy as much as it was Annie's enemy, and the snowshoes they had fabricated would make the walking faster, and with the snowshoes the walking would be less fatiguing, hence they could cover greater distance.

Rourke's eyes scanned the snow, Paul fanning to the left, his eyes on the snow and ice as well. It was futile, but the only chance, the only option, searching for some footprint, some sign the terrain had been disturbed. With the cessation of the wind, and if Annie was moving toward the mountains, fresh tracks might be possible—might. The chance of finding them was even slimmer.

Paul shouted. "John!"

Rourke turned toward the younger man, his friend, watching as Paul ran several yards west, Rourke starting after him, Paul's run in the snowshoes reminiscent of the moonwalks of the American astronauts—how long ago? Rourke thought for an instant.

Paul dropped to one knee, then shouted, "Nothing— I—I thought—"

"Keep looking—we'll find her," Rourke called back, angling back toward his earlier course, his eyes scanning the snow. Natalia would be flying north, then cutting an arc into the mountains toward which he and Paul now walked. If Annie was ahead of them and no tracks were found, Sarah with the binoculars or Natalia with the naked eye would see her—he hoped, he prayed.

He glanced at the Rolex on his left wrist, his storm

sleeve rolled back. It was three o'clock and the light would soon be fading. If she had found no shelter, she would not survive the night. Rourke quickened his pace, glancing at Paul. Paul was doing the same . . .

The Rolex read four-eighteen. When Rourke looked up from it, he saw an impression, or perhaps only a darker splotch, in the snow a few yards to his right.

He didn't call to Paul, removing his sunglasses, walking toward it slowly, his eyes focusing on it. He dropped to his right knee. "Paul!" It was the impression partially filled with snow, of a combat boot heel. "Paul!"

Rourke stood, eyeballing the direction the footprint would have come from, hearing, not hearing, the *slooshing* sound of the snowshoes in the snow, Rourke replacing his sunglasses, looking toward the high rocks some two hundred yards to the east.

"What—holy—"

"Uh-huh—you figure direction—I make it almost due north from here—follow out along a zigzag—don't miss anything. I'm backtracking up into that ridge—see if I find evidence she spent the night there—or anything else."

"Hey," Paul whispered, his voice muffled sounding, his mouth, like Rourke's, covered with the lower portion of an identical black SAS Headover. "You be careful."

"I always am," Rourke nodded, clapping Paul on the shoulder, then starting up toward the ridge, unslinging the M-16, not charging the chamber, but holding the weapon in his gloved right fist. The light—what there was—was gray now, grayer than before, darkness coming too quickly. He called back. "Two shots—pause—then two—means come fast."

"Right." Paul answered, Rourke walking on, scanning the ground. Nothing.

He found a second impression—a deep impression, cylindrical in shape, extending perhaps two inches into the snow, to the ice below it and the harder packed snow, Rourke exploring the impression with his Gerber, resheathing it, quickening his pace.

Another footprint, all but obscured—but a different footprint, the heel narrower, but much larger, the impression deeper in the snow. "A man," Rourke whispered.

He charged the M-16, working the bolt, letting it fly forward, but the selector still on safe.

He was climbing into higher rocks, a deeper darkness ahead of and above him than shadow would have created. He worked the safety tumbler to auto, his gloved right index finger alongside the trigger guard, his right fist tight on the pistol grip. "Annie!"

His own voice reverberated off the rocks, but there was no answering call.

"Annie!"

No answer. He was nearing the dark spot in the rocks—it appeared to be the mouth of a cave.

A ledge of rock—wide enough, but ice-coated, Rourke uncertain of the contour, lay ahead. Rourke worked the M-16's safety back to the on position, edging along the rock ledge.

"Annie." He didn't shout now, but called the name in a normal tone. "It's me—Daddy."

Nothing. He stopped, halfway across the rock ledge, listening, looking back into the lower terrain he had just left. He could barely see Paul, but he could track Paul easily enough, the bootprints fresh.

He edged along the ledge, working the safety to off as he neared the cave mouth.

"If you're in there, don't be frightened—just me. Been worried about you."

Rourke stepped through, into the cave mouth, stabbing the M-16 toward the deeper darkness, making himself a target. But nothing.

He shifted the rifle to his left hand, reaching his right arm back to a side pouch of the backpack. His Kel-Lite—but rather than the Dura-Cell batteries he always used, the German duplicates of the five-centuries-old D-cell, the Kel-Lite's bulb substituted as well, the five-centuries-more-modern one more brilliant. He flicked on the light, shining it into the cave.

Remnants of a fire, but brick-like objects rather than wood. He approached the fire pit, his eyes scanning the cave in the cone of light from his right hand.

He shut off the flashlight. The brick-light objects still glowed. He had no idea of their chemical composition, but he doubted the fire was more than a few hours old.

He cut the switch for the Kel-Lite back on, quickly examining the cave floor. He scanned the ceiling—ice, but some of the ice almost translucent, as though recently melted and refrozen.

Rourke closed the light, then removed his sunglasses, starting back toward the mouth of the cave.

He started out, down toward the lower elevation, already Paul out of sight, darkness closing rapidly. He put his sunglasses away in the case he sometimes used, the case hardened to guard against breakage.

He set the flashlight down beside him as he crouched, thinking as he removed the M-16's thirty-round magazine, working the bolt back, popping the chambered round. He dry-snapped the trigger, tugging down the head covering from over his mouth, biting off his right glove. His hand steamed. He clutched the right glove beneath his left armpit to hold the warmth inside as he methodically replaced the top round into the magazine lips, whacking the magazine against the gloved palm of his left hand, then replacing it up the well of the M-16.

Annie. A man with her. The man using some sort of staff for support. No sign of the survival knife Natalia theorized Annie would have taken, so perhaps Annie still had it. If she did, then the man with the staff was not an immediate, recognizable enemy — perhaps. Unless he had taken the knife.

Rourke started to his feet, but stopped. He smelled something.

He shone the flashlight to his right — against the side of the cave mouth, where snow had drifted against the opening. The snow was yellow.

Rourke stood up, mentally aiming — a man would have urinated higher along the drift, otherwise risking urinating all over his feet.

An animal.

Rourke used the flashlight, his right hand cold, bare as it was against the aircraft-aluminum tube of the flashlight — a few feet out from the cave mouth. He dropped to his knees.

It was the paw print of a dog — or a wolf.

Chapter Twelve

Paul Rubenstein dropped to his right knee—in the beam of the German flashlight, he saw another footprint, but this not Annie's, another of the larger, heavier footprints. A man. Near to it, another of the mysterious cylindrical impressions in the snow. He pulled off his glove, sticking his finger down inches into the snow—a staff? He wondered.

"Annie! Annie!"

There was no answer.

He shone his flashlight ahead, the sky starless, overcast. But a wall of gray, lighter gray than the night, ahead. One of the innumerable geysers, he thought. But the footprints led toward it. To his feet. Paul started ahead, the M-16 in his right hand, the glove back on, the flashlight in his left. "Annie!"

The flashlight was the only means to truly see; when he turned it off nothing but deep gray shadow surrounded him.

With the light, he walked ahead, searching for more footprints now, but the direction little changed since he had begun to follow the trail.

He stopped—a dark object. He approached it, slowly.

He dropped to his knees near it, studying it in the light. Fecal material. But, here in the open, like something a wild animal would leave, not a person. He remembered before the sky had caught fire, John showing him deer sign. It was like that. He stood, touching at it with the tip of his snowshoe—it was hard. He stepped back from it.

A footprint. The man. The woman's inside it— "Annie," he whispered. Beside the woman's footprint— his gloved finger more deeply traced the outline. One of the posts his father had been assigned to—they had had a large dog. An Irish Setter—but this footprint was larger. He remembered the dog running with him into the snow.

"Wolf?" Rubenstein whispered to himself and the night. Such a creature should not exist anymore. But if it did . . .

He started ahead, more quickly now, toward the steam cloud that rose like a wall.

The terrain steepened, Paul leaning into the climb, the snowshoes making it tougher going, but not something he could abandon, the snow less deep here, the ice slicker—wind-polished, he imagined.

A man should not have been here in this dead land. A wolf or a large dog—such was an impossibility.

The wind was starting up, and in the sky, at the horizon line, there were flashes of light. He let his mind wander as he climbed. The terrain, the temperature, the absence of sun, the man, the dog or wolf—it was alien, unearthly.

A land of the dead, perhaps, instead of a dead land? What if somehow the dead had all come to Iceland— the dead people, the dead animals? He laughed at the thought—dead things didn't leave footprints in the snow, nor did they need to defecate as whatever the creature was—dog or wolf—had evidently done.

He considered Annie—a pleasanter thought.

She genuinely loved him, wanted to be with him, to

be his.

In actual lived time, it had been less than a year since he had boarded the flight in Canada to get back down to the United States somehow, to somehow get back to New York—and The Night of The War had begun.

He had always been a disappointment to his father, he had known. Slight of build, not physically powerful or imposing, not interested in pursuing a military career as his father had in the Air Force. A disappointment to his mother. Twenty-eight years old, not married—but he had been engaged. He remembered Ruth's face—and he felt very cold. No one else alive would remember Ruth's face. He had met her again after knowing her as a child, at one of the rare social functions he had attended that was sponsored by his Temple. Afterward, he had taken her out for a drink. They had talked. He had called her the next day—they had begun to see each other.

Ruth had been very traditional. And he supposed so was he, or had been then. You didn't have sex unless there was a marriage first. And you got to know each other well before you got serious. You met her parents. You talked with her father. "So—you're a magazine editor?"

"Only an associate editor. But I'm learning a lot."

"You went to college?"

"Yes sir." He had started to say where, but Ruth's father hadn't let him finish.

"And your father's some kind of Air Force officer?"

"He's retired, sir—but yes—ahh—" He had started to give his father's rank, but Ruth's father hadn't let him finish.

"My Ruth—she likes you."

"I like Ruth a lot, sir."

"Let's just suppose—you know—you and my Ruth—

95

you both get serious."

"I think, ahh—we are serious, sir."

"My Ruth's a good girl."

"I don't mean that way, sir—but we care a lot about—"

Her father had laughed. "Young people. Listen—this associate editor thing you do—what did you train for in your college?"

"Journalism, sir."

"Like newspapers and magazines?"

"Yes sir."

"What if people stop buying your magazine? Then what?"

"Well—I don't know, ahh—I suppose—"

"Yeah—I suppose—my Ruth's working. My wife never worked—Ruth's mother helps out in the store sure, raised Ruth and her two brothers and her sister Marlene but she never worked."

"Well, I mean—all of that—that's work, isn't it, sir?"

"You getting smart?"

"No, Mr. Blumenthal. But I mean—well—Ruth wouldn't have to work, unless she wanted to."

"Young girls—sometimes they don't know what they want. They think they know what they want. She's only twenty-two. How old are you? Thirty-five?"

Paul had smiled uncomfortably. It was the thinning hair and the glasses—always that. "No sir—I'm twenty-eight. Ahh—it's just that my hair thins—I guess it's from my mother's father—he was bald at thirty. Least I'm not that bad yet, Mr. Blumenthal."

"Twenty-eight? Humph—you don't look twenty-eight."

"No, Mr. Blumenthal—I know that. Ruth's a wonderful girl. And I'd like your permission to go on seeing her."

"And what would you do if I don't give it to you?"

"I'd ask Ruth to keep seeing me anyway, Mr. Blumenthal—being honest. And I'd hope you'd change your mind, sir."

"Bullshit—find yourself a real job. Go ahead—see my Ruth. But find yourself a real job."

"It is a real job, sir—honest."

He had walked Ruth around the block three times, then taken her up, kissed her good-night, and told her that he loved her. She had told him that she loved him.

The next day he had flown to Canada.

Paul Rubenstein reached the top of the rise, shining his flashlight down toward where the steam was more concentrated. He thought he saw—"Holy—"

Chapter Thirteen

Natalia looked at the ladies' Rolex on her left wrist. "In an hour, we'll go up."

"Akiro should be here by then," Sarah said from across the lamp.

"Yes. But it's too dark to search. John should fire a flare at eight p.m. — then another at eight-fifteen, and another at eight-thirty if I haven't picked them up by then."

"You think they found Annie?" Sarah whispered.

"I don't know. I pray they did." And Natalia laughed at herself. "Who could I pray to?"

"What do you mean?" Sarah asked her.

"I mean — I'm part Jewish, part Christian — I have never gone to any kind of church — except on assignments — following someone, making a drop — like that."

"What was it like? I mean — well —"

"To be a major in the KGB?"

Sarah nodded, saying nothing. Natalia watched as Sarah pulled the blue and white bandanna from her hair, shaking it loose. Natalia leaned back, almost warm inside the helicopter, her coat open, her gunbelt beside her. "What was it like? Well — did John ever have you sleep with a man to get information for him?"

"No," Sarah answered, her voice barely audible.

"Vladmir — he had me do that. He told me, 'Natalia—it is for the good of the people of the Soviet.' "

"Did you believe him?" Sarah asked.

"I think I did."

"Then you didn't do anything wrong."

"How do you know?" Natalia whispered.

"What?"

"How do you know—that I didn't do anything wrong, I mean."

"Well, I mean—you did it for what you thought were the right reasons, and—"

"I killed people. I never tortured people—but I knew Vladmir was doing it. I never stopped him, Sarah."

"Is that what you were doing when you met John?"

Natalia closed her eyes, still seeing the glare of the lamp despite her lids covering her eyes. "Did John never tell you?"

"He never spoke about his missions other than to say it went well or it didn't."

Natalia laughed, still not opening her eyes. "For your husband, it almost invariably went well. That was why Vladmir set the trap for him and tried to kill him. John was too successful." She squeezed her eyes more tightly shut, remembering—the first time she had seen his face. Sweat-stained, muddy, his hair uncombed, a days' growth of beard on his face, an empty .45 automatic in his fist. Wounded.

"What are you thinking?" Sarah asked her quietly.

Natalia opened her eyes. "Maybe about who I pray to," and she smiled . . .

It was animal fecal matter. John Rourke shone the light away from it, toward the snowshoe prints of Paul Rubenstein. Paul was following to the left of the footprints of Annie, the dog or wolf, and the man with the staff, following up along a slope toward the gray-

99

white steam of a geyser, Rourke assumed.

He started after him.

For some reason, he thought about Captain Dodd, Commander of the Eden Fleet. There was a fundamental difference between Dodd and himself. Dodd came at everything, or so it seemed, Rourke admitted, from the negative. John Rourke had always accepted the negative as being there, and had chosen to come at things from the positive. Any rational man with an adequate understanding of the effects of hypothermia would have concluded that Annie was dead. Such a rational observation did not escape John Rourke, but he simply refused to accept it until reality gave him no choice. His father had told him something once that, unlike most advice, he had taken to heart. "John—you ever think about what makes a man or woman, or a nation—what makes them succeed when others fail?"

"Well—you mean one special quality?"

"Yeah—think about it. We'll talk about it later." And his father had put in his earplugs and drawn a fresh loaded .45 ACP magazine from the waistband of his trousers and loaded it up the butt of his Colt Government Model. John Rourke had put in his own earplugs, watching as his father shot. Unlike John Rourke, John Rourke's father had been truly ambidextrous. John Rourke had taught himself ambidexterity, but his father was even-handed—in more ways than one, Rourke thought now, scaling the slope, his snowshoes off, slung over his shoulder by the bindings. His father had fired one magazine with the right hand, then, with the slide locked open, changed magazines, shifted to his left hand, worked the slide release down with his left first finger, and continued shooting.

The targets were cans of peas, empty, his mother saving cans from peas, beans, all kinds of vegetables for his father's and later his own target practice.

Another seven cans were shot off the rail and tumbled to the ground after a brief, and, at John Rourke's age, spectacular-seeming journey skyward.

His father set the .45 down, but didn't remove his earplugs so John Rourke had known there would be more shooting soon. John Rourke had fired revolvers from the age of five, starting with his father's Smith & Wesson .357 Magnum, one of the few .357 Magnums relatively speaking that had been available before World War II, something the elder Rourke had kept as a target pistol before the war, then broken out to use after the war had ended when ammunition had become available for it again.

This was the first day his father had hinted at him shooting the .45. His father, shouting as he always did when he wore ear protection, said, "John—wanna try it?"

John Rourke was ten years old.

"Yeah—sure, Dad."

"Okay—now I know you know this, but I'm going to tell you again. Every time you pull the trigger and a round discharges, that slide is going to come back fast, so fast you really can't see it. But if your thumb or the web of your hand—this part"—and he touched his son's hand between the thumb and first finger—"gets in the way, well—it hurts. Okay."

"Yeah—okay," and his father had loaded a fresh magazine into the .45, worked down the slide release and upped the safety, the hammer at full stand.

"You get a stoppage or a failure to fire, just keep it pointed downrange—I'll be right beside you. Settle your hand comfortably and work the safety down—before you put your finger into the trigger guard. Got me?"

"Yeah."

"Go for it," and he had handed John Rourke the .45.

101

Rourke settled the pistol in his hand, the elder Rourke beside him. He worked down the thumb safety, holding the pistol tight to keep the grip safety properly depressed. He looked to see that his hand was clear of the slide. He touched the trigger. A can went sailing skyward, then fell.

The next two shots were misses, putting bullet holes in the rail. The distance was something like ten yards. The next two shots after that were hits. Then a miss. One shot remained and Rourke made a conscious effort to control his breathing, steady his hand. He wanted to get the can with the last shot — very badly. He touched the trigger gently, the .45 discharging — the can never moved.

The slide was locked open and he kept the pistol downrange but turned to look up at his father. His father pulled out the earplugs, then took the .45, working the stop down, ramming the pistol between his shirt and his trouser band. It was a white shirt, his tie down, his vest open, the earplugs going into a little transparent canister and then into his vest pocket.

John Rourke removed his earplugs. His father put a hand to John Rourke's shoulder and looked down at him. "So — you shot pretty well — need some more practice, though. I watched you on that last shot. You gave it everything you had, right?"

"Right. But I still missed."

"You gonna try again?"

"Sure — soon as you let me."

"You just answered that question — about why some people, some nations, succeed when others fail."

John Rourke had looked into his father's brown eyes, saying, "I don't understand."

"Sure you do — think about it." His father had lit a cigarette, then smiled. "Think about that last shot you tried."

"You mean—ahh—well—you just gotta keep trying, Dad?"

"Yeah—that's what I mean. You never give up. If something needs doing you just keep trying to do it—either the job will get done or you'll die in the process, but either way, you never give up. Okay?" And he had run his left hand through his son's hair, then grabbed him about the shoulders and given him a hug. "Okay?"

"Yeah," John Rourke had smiled. "Yeah."

When his father had died, John Rourke stood over the gravesite, the last person to leave it, saying, "I won't give up, Dad," and had taken a handful of dirt and thrown it into the grave.

John Rourke reached the summit of the slope, peering down into the cloud of steam.

He had learned something else from his father, and his mother too—to trust his own powers of reason.

John Rourke whispered to the night surrounding him, "My God."

Chapter Fourteen

"We have received a radio communication from the Underground City, Comrade Marshal Karamatsov."

"Sit down."

Krakovski sat down, placing his hat on the table, Antonovitch looking at him.

Krakovski spoke again. "Most peculiar, really."

Karamatsov stared at the young major—there had been no colonlecy for either Krakovski or Antonovitch, Rourke turning what had seemed undoubted victory into a rout. It had to have been Rourke. The yellow light of the lamp made shadows on the wall of the hut, the West Texas wind howling loudly enough that Karamatsov could not get it from his brain, listening to it. "What is so peculiar?"

"A distress beacon, Comrade Marshal—identical to that of our gunships. Triangulation was made, fixing its position—I have the coordinates—but near the southwest coast of Iceland."

"Iceland?"

Krakovski looked at Antonovitch, "Yes, Comrade—Iceland."

Antonovitch murmured, "Perhaps one of the gunships lost to the Eden Project fleet. But why Iceland?"

Karamatsov had never concerned himself with technology. "Could the distress signal have been triggered accidentally?"

"Highly dubious, Comrade Marshal—no. But who would have sent it?"

"From the tone of your voice," Karamatsov hissed, "you apparently have a suggestion, Major."

"Yes, Comrade Marshal—I do. Iceland was a Western Ally, of sorts at least. Perhaps the Americans stored equipment there, or weapons. Iceland, according to one radical theory, may have been spared the global destruction when the sky caught fire."

"What are you talking about? Why was I never told this?"

"Comrade Marshal—it is a radical theory, only. But the basis of it, in layman's terms, was that there was a shift in the Van Allen belts, and the charged particles which caused the ionization effect that burned away the bulk of the atmosphere would have been decreased by the solar winds. That in effect, the normal atmospheric mixing would have been blocked, and what amounts to a shield would have been present to insulate Iceland and some other polar regions against the destruction of its immediate atmosphere, preserving an atmosphere there."

"What?"

"That is the theory, Comrade Marshal," Krakovski smiled, shrugging his shoulders, "But of course, no life would have survived. The extreme cold of those days. In the polar regions, the temperatures are believed to have dropped by as much as—"

"I don't really care. You believe the Americans might have valuable equipment stored in Iceland, having foreseen this thing with the—"

"The Van Allen belts, Comrade Marshal—and yes, the possibility exists."

Antonovitch shook his head. "Such a theory might account for the more rapid reforestation in the northern portions of what was Canada—this we have observed—not all the oxygen was perhaps burned away. And with the polar shift—the temperature in our own northern lands have been warmer than corresponding areas in Canada in similar latitudes."

Marshal Vladmir Karamatsov considered, staring away from Krakovski and Antonovitch into his tented fingers. "These Van Allen belts—I have heard of them, of course. But exactly how could they have such an effect, Krakovski? I make no pretense to scientific knowledge in any great depth. In the field, there was little time for reading scholarly journals."

Krakovski cleared his throat. "Of course, Comrade Marshal. Basically," and he exhaled loudly, "the theory propounded suggested that the essentially equatorially-based Van Allen radiation belts were artificially expanding as more and more charged nuclear particles were shifting from artificial radiation belts caused by the various thermonuclear explosions into the fields of the established belts. The belts are distorted in the normal course of events by the pressures of the solar winds. It is likely that protons and electrons from the solar winds reacted with the charged particles in the belts. The theory is that some portions of the earth were spared by virtue of the peculiar inequities of the magnetosphere. Only on rare occasions during freak magnetic storms—such as occurred the morning of the devastation—would the proton density of the lower belt be altered drastically, while normally the electron population of the outer belt would be affected significantly by such storms. The magnetic anomaly took place." Krakovski shrugged his shoulders and smiled, surrendering his hands, palms upward. "Just as this served to destroy life on earth, the bow shock wave may have been so powerful—one mustn't forget the interaction with the auroral zone—that this . . . shield, as it were, was established. No vacuum was formed, of course, when the oxygen was burned off, but rather the space occupied by the oxygen was filled by gases resulting from the general conflagration that consumed the surface. In essence, a portion of the earth's atmosphere was positively charged, another negatively charged, and a portion of the atmosphere was very warm, another very cold. There was no mix — or so the theory goes. I too am a military man, and have little knowledge of scientific matters. Perhaps I could arrange for a dispatch to be sent from the Underground City explaining the potential for the anomaly?"

Vladmir Karamatsov studied Krakovski's face a moment, having understood next to nothing of the man's words. But he made a decision. "Major Krakovski — you will take a small but adequate force and travel by the most expeditious route toward this set of coordinates in Iceland. You will report to me immediately concerning your findings. If by some means the Americans have taken possession of a cache of weapons or other strategic material, you may be called upon to destroy these items or seize them." Karamatsov still studied Krakovski's face. "Should by any chance the American Rourke be involved — or my wife — you will take whatever steps needed to ensure their elimination if necessary, their capture if possible, but their neutralization at any cost."

Krakovski stood to attention, saying, "My forces await, Comrade Marshal!"

"How nice," Karamatsov murmured. "How very nice." And he looked away, hearing Krakovski exit the hut. Krakovski was a very ambitious man — very.

Chapter Fifteen

John Rourke had removed his backpack in order to lash the snowshoes more properly to the pack to prevent incidental noise. He was perched on a ledge of black volcanic rock, clouds of steam surrounding him. He made a decision, his eyes searching the semi-darkness here — he found a niche in the rock and started toward it, hiking the pack into his left hand.

He set the pack into the niche, opening it. He unzipped his coat, slowly opening the velcro storm closure over the zipper to reduce noise. He shrugged out of the coat, seating himself in the niche, unblousing his snow pants, zipping open the leg closures and doffing them quickly. His leather jacket was back aboard the German helicopter. But it was warm here.

The faded blue Levis were light for the work ahead, but would have to do. He left the gray crewneck sweater in place, comfortable enough with it. He pulled off the SAS Headover, stuffing it into the sleeve of his coat, his gloves beside it, only the thinner gloves that he normally used still with him. From the top of his pack, he took the full-flap holster for the Python, buckling it on, checking the cylinder, closing the cylinder, holstering the Python. He had left the Score-masters with Natalia and Sarah, but besides the Python and the M-16, for which he had only three spare magazines, he had the twin stainless Detonics mini-guns in the double Alessi shoulder rig over his sweater. There was no need to check them—he knew their condition of readiness. From the pack, he took the Sparks Six-Pack for the little Detonics magazines, threading it into its customary position on his pants belt, reclosing the belt. He patted the Gerber knife on his pistol belt, felt for the little A.G. Russell Sting IA black chrome on his right side, inside the pants. His sunglasses—he took the case and checked the glasses inside, then dropped the case into the musette bag with his spare M-16 magazines. He grabbed up his cigar case, putting it with the sunglasses and the magazines.

He closed the pack, shoving it back further into the niche, lashing his coat and snowpants to it. He might have to leave in a hurry. Some emergency medical supplies were in the musette bag—they would have to do. With them an unbroken box of fifty rounds of Federal 185-grain jacketed hollowpoints, a few spare Detonics magazines, and his compass. The compass was next-to-useless here.

He stared down through the steam. He remembered something now. The map had referred to this mountain as the dormant volcano Mt. Hekla, and he remembered something he had read years ago concerning Iceland—that Mt. Hekla was surrounded once in legend, thought to be one of the gates into hell.

Dimly, through the great clouds of white steam, he could see lights. Something was down there, inside the volcano. And Paul Rubenstein's tracks had ended here, as had Annie's tracks, the tracks of the wolf or dog—a hound of hell? he smiled to himself—and the tracks of the man with the staff, perhaps a devil with an inverted pitchfork.

John Rourke didn't really care if it was hell or

something else.

He started down into the volcano — to find his daughter and his best friend, the M-16 tight in his right fist, tensioned against its sling . . .

There was a standard rule of thumb with Icelandic- or Hawaiian-type shield volcanoes — the base diameter was generally approximately twenty times the height of the volcano. Hekla, if he recalled data from the topographic maps, seemed to be four-fifths of a mile high, making the base diameter approximately eighty thousand feet — just shy of sixteen miles. The craters of shield volcanoes characteristically had slopes angling between three and eight degrees, the crater steep-walled and the base flat, the result what was termed a pit crater.

Rourke had scaled the sides of the pit for some twenty minutes, perhaps fifteen — he had lost track of the time, obsessed with staring beneath him. There would be regular paths, of course, a vastly simpler means of descending, but regular paths might be traveled even late in the evening. He kept to his course, the harder way but the surer way.

A community — he was reminded of the small, seemingly untouched community in Bevington, Kentucky, where he had nearly lost his life.

The clouds of steam were less dense as he descended — a warm air source, and as the steam rose it grew more dense with the cold, he surmised. He could see clearly at times, and now, as he stopped on a spit of volcanic rock, stripped away the double Alessi shoulder rig, then peeled away the crewneck sweater, he studied what appeared below him.

Gardens. Trees. Pathways rather than streets. Flowers in what from the distance appeared as well-manicured beds.

Dwellings. The houses were square — symmetrical, really — with peaked roofs slanting off pyramidally downward. Solid-looking; gray, white, or tan in color, it seemed. Electric arc lamps illuminated the pathways in purple lights — giant-sized grow lights. The entire image seemed somehow terrarium-like.

It was not hell.

He tied the sweater around his neck because there was no other place to put it, his double shoulder rig back in place. He kept descending. No people seemed evident along the paths, but with the intermittent breaks in the steam clouds his windows to the world below, it was impossible to speak with certainty, he knew.

He kept going, downward, the ambient temperature into the upper sixties or lower seventies in degrees Fahrenheit, he speculated. He stopped again, rolling up the sleeves of his blue chambray shirt to just below the elbows. He kept the gloves on to protect his hands against the rock. He kept going.

John Rourke continued the descent for another ten minutes — this time he had made himself consciously note the time. He stopped again, less than a hundred yards above the flat expanse that stretched before him. He glanced at his left wrist, to the Rolex there — it was already after nine p.m. He had missed the signal contact with Natalia, and he would miss the next signal and the one after that — unless he climbed up out of the volcano's crater.

And time might be precious. He would rely on Natalia and Sarah to take whatever logical course of action presented itself.

He continued downward, more slowly now, cautious lest he dislodge a rock and make some betraying noise. Such a place would surely have at least minimal

111

security. His mind raced as he descended, his eyes squinting against the purple light of the pathway lamps. A human habitation, warmth, almost subtropical lushness of vegetation—but in, at the least, a subarctic region.

The presence of geothermal energy was obvious—the hot water that vented steam into the crater. Natural geothermal wells could have provided heat, steam to power the turbines for electricity, the heat sufficient to convert the entire crater base into an uncovered greenhouse. The grow lights would be used throughout the Arctic night with its total absence or paucity of sunlight. When the grow lights died, they would be replaced, geothermal energy again harnessed to power the factory that made them. At the far side of the crater he had glimpsed larger structures—perhaps the factories, perhaps government buildings.

A rationale for the present existence of the community unfolding before his eyes was perfectly within the realm of the possible, but where had the people come from who'd built and maintained it? As he drew closer to the volcano floor, it was clear that the flower beds were worked regularly, the grass into which they were set regularly cut. Plant debris could be used to create alcohol, another fuel source—for additional machinery.

But how had people come to be here?

John Rourke froze, his left foot in air only, his right hand and right foot perched on a ledge of rock some twelve feet above the flat surface below. It was clear the surface had been engineered.

And it was one of the engineers now that he saw, heard. He drew back, slowly, up onto the ledge.

A man. Another a few steps behind him, at each man's left hip a sword hilt and scabbard. One man's hair was red, his beard red. The other's, long and

112

bearded as well, had a straw-blond color. They wore leather-looking nearly-knee-high boots, green pants bloused above the boot tops, sleeveless tunics extending to their knees, the tunics green, beneath the tunics shirts with baggy sleeves, green also. The fronts of the tunics were cut low to the waist, the sword belt cinching the tunic, the green shirtfront visible beneath the tunic.

Except for the absence of horned helmets and shields and their spotless-seeming cleanliness, they looked like movie-lot Vikings.

Policemen? Rourke wondered.

The men were walking past him, almost directly below him. The red-haired man was at least six foot two and the blond-haired was an inch or so taller, both of them well over two hundred pounds, but apparently well-muscled beneath the theatrical-looking costumes.

He could call to them—but chances were that they spoke Icelandic if they spoke anything recognizable, and though, as he recalled, Icelandic bore interesting similarities to Old and Middle English, he doubted they would understand him or he them.

No guns—at least none visible.

Rourke considered calling to them merely to get their attention and aiming the M-16 at them—but if they lacked the concept of guns, they might not apprehend his meaning.

And it might be unwise and at this point most probably purposeless to kill.

John Rourke unslung the M-16 and his musette bag as quietly as he could, setting them back behind him on the spit of rock outcropping on which he was crouched.

The men passed beneath him—Rourke jumped, his hands and arms reaching out, grabbing at both of the green Vikings, bulldogging them to the ground, the blond coming up in a roll, the red-haired man flat on the flagstone pathway, Rourke to his knees, dodging left as the blond-haired man lunged for him, Rourke rocking onto his left knee and hand, his right foot shooting up, avoiding the groin, going for the solar plexus, the blond doubling forward, dropping to his knees as Rourke fell away from him. To his feet now. The redhead snarled as he tried to stand up, Rourke's gloved right fist hammering outward and upward, arcing through a classic uppercut, the knuckles of his right fist screaming at him when bone contacted bone, the redhead's head snapping back, the body going limp, sprawling into the grass. Rourke wheeled, the blond coming at him again. Rourke feigned another savate kick, rotated one hundred eighty degrees, and made a double tae kwan do kick to the right ribcage and right upper arm of the charging blond.

The redhead was up, reaching for his sword. Rourke hurtled himself toward the man, a martial-arts attack that was impossible to wholly defend against, both fists hammering toward the man, the right knee poised for a smash—but concurrent with it was the chance of getting hit. As Rourke's left fist smashed against the redhead's right cheekbone, his right knee impacting the abdomen just above the testicles, the green-clad Viking's right fist backhanded off the sword hilt, catching Rourke along the right side of the jawline, the redhead stumbling away, Rourke falling to his knees. He rolled as the redhead recovered faster than he—Rourke—did, a sweeping kick coming toward Rourke's face. But Rourke caught the foot in both hands, throwing his body weight into the leg, then down, the redhead screaming. If he had a weak knee, it was dislocated. Rourke was up on his feet, the redhead screaming at him in something wholly incomprehensible to Rourke, his right hand with the sword half out of the sheath.

Rourke wheeled half-right, his left foot snapping out, impacting the base of the redhead's jaw with the toe of his combat boot. The green-clad redhead slumped back, eyelids fluttering. Rourke wheeled full-right, the blond coming at him, the sword in a downswing.

Rourke hurled himself across the redhead, grasping for the sword.

He rolled as the blond's sword cleaved air above him.

To his feet, but now Rourke had the redhead's sword and stood with its ornate hilt in both fists, poised. The blond took a step back, then lunged.

The blond raised the sword with his right hand, whipping the sword upward and then presenting the blade's tip toward Rourke—some sort of salute, Rourke surmised.

Rourke took a step back, watching the blond's eyes—they were riveted to the big Gerber MkII at Rourke's left hip. Rourke shifted the balance of the sword, holding it with one hand, drawing the Gerber with his left hand. The blond still eyed it.

Rourke gathered somehow it wasn't gentlemanly to have a dagger available when the other fellow didn't. Rourke hefted the Gerber, then flipped it. It wasn't a throwing knife, and in most cases throwing a knife was the least practical option. But he pitched it toward the grass, the blade biting into the dirt, staying.

He looked at the blond and nodded, the blond nodding back. As the blond started toward him, Rourke sidestepped, right, the sword pointed downward bisecting the line of his left upper arm. Then Rourke sidestepped right again, as if crossing into his opponent's path, but Rourke held the sword with the blade bisecting the line of his throat, the tip to Rourke's right, his blade parallel now to his shoulders, blocking the blond's downward hacking attack with the full force of his body, their blades locking.

Rourke stepped back with his left foot, making the wedge of his body a more solid block against the blond-haired man, Rourke's arms upthrusting, the blond leaning into the blade, slightly off balance, his weight too far forward. Rourke pivoted thirty degrees with his right foot, throwing the weight to his right leg, flexing the knee. Rourke snapped his left foot up and forward, the toe of his combat boot impacting the blond man's scrotum, the blond's china-blue eyes dilating for an instant with pain.

The blond took a wobbling step back, their blades still locked, Rourke's left foot down now, moving forward, their blades parting, Rourke hacking his own blade downward and right, the swords locked against the wide double quillon guards, Rourke knocking his opponent's blade right and down. Rourke shifted his weight to his left foot, pulling his right leg behind him as if pivoting one hundred eighty degrees, but instead, their blades still locked at the level of Rourke's abdomen, Rourke snapped his left elbow up, his elbow contacting the partially-doubled-forward blond-haired man's chin. Rourke's left fist released the hilt of the sword, the heel of his left fist snapping forward, catapulting against the center of the blond-haired man's forehead just above the nose. His weight still on his right foot, his blade still blocking his opponent's blade, Rourke's left foot snapped outward in a side kick, against the right outside and rear of his opponent's right knee, Rourke's left fist backhanding cross-body into the blond's lower left jawline, the blond's head snapping right, the blond's hands releasing the sword, the sword clattering to the flagstones of the path. Rourke swung his sword in a left arc with his right hand, loosing the hilt, the sword implanting into the ground near the Gerber knife. The blond's body was limping, starting down as Rourke's right knee smashed up, impacting the base of the blond man's jaw.

The head snapped back, the body back-flipping into the flower bed.

It had been a long time since John Rourke had practiced his kendo — at least five centuries.

Chapter Sixteen

John Rourke had debated waiting around for one of them to awaken, to try all possible variants of "girl," "woman," "female," and "daughter" to see if there was a flash of recognition.

Instead he left the bodies where they fell, and clambered up into the rocks, getting his M-16 and his musette bag.

Once back down, he had debated taking the sword the red-haired man had involuntarily loaned him — but to have defeated the blond-haired man in combat was one thing, to take his sword would dishonor him. Blade-oriented cultures were high in the attachment of honor to their weapons, historically at least. But, Rourke reflected, if someone had taken his twin stainless Detonics pistols, it would have sat poorly with him as well.

He checked both men — both unconscious, both breathing satisfactorily. He retrieved his Gerber, leaving the men, running along the path now, his M-16 at high port. Viking warriors living in a place that by right should not exist — a technologically sophisticated place, so sophisticated that the need for blatant demonstration of the level of sophistication was apparently thought unnecessary. When he had retrieved his knife, the ground had felt warm, warmer than it should have felt considering the air temperature and the outside environment.

Pipes, he presumed, were laid out along the ground, heating it. The energy requirements would be enormous, but the raw material for the energy, water, was recyclable with the exception of what he now realized was the comparatively small amount that escaped as steam.

He kept running. Annie was here. Paul was here . . .

Paul Rubenstein moved ahead along the ground on knees and elbows, stopping behind a hedgerow and listening. The language spoken by the long-skirted, fit-seeming, and very pretty girls was totally alien to him, all but for a trace of something that reminded him vaguely of segments of *Beowulf* in the original Old English that he had been exposed to once in college.

He had enjoyed the translation, in fact had re-read *Beowulf* several times — the first adventure novel, a professor had called it, as well as the oldest extant work in English.

The girls were seated on a low-backed wooden bench. Seated was the wrong word, perched more the term, he decided, the girls sitting on the edge of the bench, leaned forward, engrossed in their animated conversation, their skirts completely masking their legs. One girl was dark blonde, the other light blonde; one girl's hair in braids that danced as she moved her head in conversation, the other girl's hair braided as well, but the braids upswept and bound around her head — it was a hair style he had seen in old nineteenth-century photographs.

"Shit," he snarled under his breath. He rolled onto his side, undoing the belt at his waist for his pack, then shouldering first out of the left strap, then out of the right, then rolling to his left side—he opened the pack as noiselessly as he could. His flashlight. The musette bag with the spare magazines for his Browning High Power—the newer-looking spare gun he had left with Sarah and Natalia, as John Rourke had left the Scoremasters. Neither of them had expected battle. He took the second musette bag—spare magazines for the Schmeisser. He had two spare magazines for the M-16, taking them and shoving them into his hip pockets now. The flashlight he shoved into his trouser waistband. He checked for the battered Browning's security in the Special Weapons Products' tanker holster—the velcro strap was closed tight.

He left the pack, pushing it as silently as he could beneath the hedgerow, trying to memorize the location—the positioning of the bench, the small, actually gurgling brook which ran perhaps ten feet to his right.

He pushed up to his knees, watching the girls a moment longer.

Who they were, why they even existed, was not immediately apparent. But he knew sophisticated technology when he saw it. The ground was warm to the touch—pleasantly so. Pipes buried within the ground, he realized. The whole place was climate-controlled with geothermal energy.

On knees and elbows, taking a last look toward his pack, Paul Rubenstein began to crawl away. Annie . . .

Natalia spoke into her headset microphone. "Sarah—do you read me? Over."

"I read you, Natalia—a little static. Over."

"I haven't sighted any flares. Either John is late or there's something wrong. Over."

"Kurinami just came in—Want me to send him up,

Natalia? Over."

Natalia's eyes scanned the night—her consciousness was somehow still drawn to the mountains toward which John and Paul had trekked in search of footprints or some slight sign of Annie. John hadn't said it—but Natalia realized it full well. If Annie spent a second night unprotected with these low temperatures, she would be dead. "No—I'll give you my position. I'm just due west of a dormant volcano marked on our maps as Mt. Hekla. There's considerable steam rising from it. I'm taking the machine down. Let Akiro rest for a while, then have Michael and Madison keep the watch at camp, have Elaine stay with them. You and Akiro come after me if you don't get a transmission from me within two hours. Understood? Natalia, over."

"Understood—be careful. And thank you—for a lot of things. Sarah out."

Natalia focused her attention toward the clouds of steam, switching on the thermal-scanning equipment of the German helicopter—the steam seemed to be emitting more heat in greater concentration than any of the geysers she had taken test readings against earlier.

She started the German helicopter down, switching on landing lights because with the overcast it was the only way she could find a landing spot. She realized that if some enemy force were out there, they would spot her because of the lights. But provoking a reaction, if such a force existed, seemed the most expeditious way of making contact. She hit the switches for full lights now, using the rotating spots. There was no sense in making it difficult . . .

Annie Rourke awoke—something like bells. An alarm—the ringing was all around her, a voice in the

121

strange language proclaiming something she couldn't understand. She pushed the covers down from her bed, throwing her feet to the floor, the nightgown that had bunched at her hips falling to her ankles now. Her feet blindly found the slippers she had been given. She found the light switch, hitting it—the bedside lamp cast a yellow glow in a cone of light beside her feet and across much of the rug. She found the six-foot-square fringed shawl on the chest at the bottom of the bed by the footboard, folding it around herself, starting for the door. She tried the door handle—it opened. They hadn't locked her in. She stepped into the hallway. People were running, other women like herself in nightdresses and shawls, men topless and barefoot, closing their pants as they ran, green-tunicked guards, their swords buckling on.

She looked right and left along the corridor, then started to run, following the greatest concentration of women . . .

Natalia stared down into the steam clouds—lights. Purplish lights. Perhaps more lavender. She pulled the hood closer about her face, tugging at the silk scarf over her mouth and nose that guarded her face at least slightly against the cold.

The sound she heard was more unnatural than the lights.

A choice—return to the helicopter and get help, or go it alone.

Emotion or logic. She chose logic, running, skidding down the slope, falling, picking herself up and slogging down through the snow. The sound was barely audible now over the rising wind. But it was some sort of loud alarm signal.

Chapter Seventeen

"Damn," John Rourke hissed, breaking out of his jog-trot and into a run. The guards might have awakened, but more likely when he had crossed one of the expanses of open ground he had broken the beam of an electronic eye or stepped on a pressure-sensitive plate. "Damn," and he threw himself into the run. Mingled with the alarm but less audible was a voice, the language something like Norwegian, but closer to Old English and totally unintelligible to him.

He kept running, breaking left, into a stand of fruit trees—peaches and apples.

He could hear voices now, shouted commands from the far side of the orchard. He kept running that way anyway—there was no other way to run unless he turned back.

Annie. Paul. John Rourke kept running, well into the orchard now, the fruit here in various stages of growth, some ripe and ready to be picked, some just flowering—a totally controlled, seasonless environment.

Smart people—he wondered if they were deadly.

He was nearing the end of the orchard now, a running man in green tunic and high boots dressed identically to the first two men, coming toward him, shouting, brandishing his sword. Rourke slowed, looked to left and right. The sword-wielding man—blond-haired, bearded, was charging still. If the rifle in Rourke's hands had been an M-1 Garand or an M-14, he would have risked using it to block the sword. But the M-16 was too fragile. As the man charged, Rourke dropped, going into a short roll, then a leg sweep, bringing the man down face forward to the bark-covered ground of the orchard, Rourke up to his knees, snapping the M-16's butt against the side of the man's head, putting him down.

The ethics of taking a man's sword left him now—he picked up the sword, identical in shape and size to the one he had used before, but the carving in the hilt different, the guard slightly different in shape. Lack of total uniformity was a good sign.

Rourke took the sword and ran with it, still heading for the far end of the orchard.

Another guard, his sword drawn running toward Rourke, shouting in the bizarre but beautiful-sounding language—he imagined it was Icelandic. He hoped.

That this was some sort of survival colony was clear—but how had they survived?

The swordsman attacked, Rourke sidestepping, one-handing his sword, countering the blow, backstepping, the swordsman cleaving downward with his blade. Rourke blocking it to the right, snapping his left fist out and forward, lacing the man across the jaw, putting him down.

Rourke ran, his M-16 bouncing across his back on its sling, the sword in his right fist.

He was out of the orchard now, into a long greenway that reminded him of the mall between the Capitol Building and the Washington Monument, running, a taller, imposing-looking building ahead of him, men pouring down the steps of the building, green-clad some of them, some of them shirtless, some wielding swords, some barehanded.

Rourke slowed, stopped.

He looked behind him. More of the same. To either side now, men coming, closing him off.

Rourke took the weapon in his right fist and hurled it away, the sword's blade burying several inches into the grassy ground.

Rourke swung the M-16 forward, working the bolt back, chambering a round, working the selector to auto.

He swung the muzzle of the rifle toward the impressive-looking building and the men running from it toward him.

He fired, into the ground a dozen yards ahead of the leaders.

The leaders slowed. Rourke fired again. They stopped.

Rourke swung the M-16 left, firing a short burst, stopping the left flank attack.

He swung the rifle behind him, to both sides—none of the men moved.

The alarm still sounded.

There was a word for it—standoff . . .

It was some sort of dormitory, half-naked men, women in long nightgowns with shawls, some few of them with robes, running from what seemed the main doors, stopping at various levels along the high steps, some of the men running down the steps, toward the more central portion of the volcano floor. What Paul Rubenstein had heard he had heard before—a .223 fired on full auto. He saw no guns in evidence, but there would be security forces, more than just the bearded, long-haired men he had observed patrolling the grounds with swords at their hips.

He knew the meaning of the concept of one's heart leaping—he felt it. Annie—in a long nightgown, a shawl wrapped about her upper body, her hair uncombed, standing near the top of the steps. Beautiful.

Paul Rubenstein broke cover, running, hurdling the hedge, running, shouting, "Annie! I'm coming for you!"

Men from the steps started toward him, one of them with a sword, the other barehanded. Paul Rubenstein fired the Schmeisser into the grass near their feet, firing another burst into the air over their heads. Annie was starting down the steps, running toward him.

The man with the sword—he moved out of his paralysis and started to charge, Paul firing into the ground at the man's feet, the man sidestepping the impact line, still running. "There's always a hardass," Paul almost verbalized, running, sidestepping as the man charged, dodging the sword, hammering the Schmeisser against the man's head, putting him down.

Paul started to lose his balance, caught himself, ran, Annie at the base of the steps now, holding the shawl clutched to her chest in her left hand, hitching up the nightgown with the fingers of her right. "Paul—don't kill anyone! Paul!"

Paul Rubenstein looked back—the swordsman, the right side of his face streaming blood, was running after him, the sword upraised, ready to strike.

Annie—Paul reached her, his left arm sweeping around her, hugging her body against him. His lips brushed at her forehead. The swordsman. Paul made to fire. "Don't kill him, Paul!"

Paul looked at her quickly—he trusted her judgment—he fired again into the ground by the swordsman's feet, making the man dodge. "Steps—come on!" He grabbed her hand, running with her now, brandishing the subgun as he started up the steps, feeling

Annie pull free of his hand, glancing toward her — her shawl, the hem of her nightgown. To the height of the steps. Paul grabbed the battered Browing High Power from the Tanker holster, thrusting it into Annie's right hand now. "Round's chambered — what the hell's going on?"

"These people — they're peaceful — one of them saved my life."

"I love you — you all right?"

"I love you too — yes — " He felt her move close against him, the Schmeisser in both his fists now. More of the assault-rifle fire from the distance.

"Can't be that peaceful."

"Maybe it's Daddy — "

"Shit — " The swordsman was racing up the steps — Paul shouted to him, "Hold it — I'll kill you — so help me!"

"They speak Icelandic — but — "

The swordsman didn't slow his pace. Annie moved, stepped in front of Paul, Paul trying to push her back. She held her left palm out toward him, clutching the pistol against the front of her shawl. "No!" She was screaming the word.

Overhead, Paul heard the sound of a chopper . . .

Natalia Anastasia Tiemerovna parted the swirling mists of steam as the German machine descended. The gunfire she had heard while making the radio transmission — it had decided her.

Her hands moved to arm the German gunship's machine guns, targeting manually, her eyes scanning the mists — purple light, more pronounced now, but definitely lavender. Gardens everywhere. Trees. A long grassy stretch amid orchards and official-looking buildings.

John Rourke, surrounded on all sides by a growing ring of men—in their hands, yes, swords, she realized. The knot around John was closing in.

She had the machine guns armed.

She hit the switch for public address, speaking into her headset microphone, realizing they wouldn't understand her, but John would. "John—this is Natalia—I'm coming in for you!"

She fired the machine guns into the ground near the ring of men—if John wasn't cutting them down, but for some reason was holding back, she would too—unless she had no choice.

The crowd started to disperse, Natalia speaking into the microphone on PA again. "Be ready, John—Akiro should be here in three minutes or less." She fired another burst from port and starboard guns, hovering, then turning the machine a full 180 degrees on its axis, starting to descend. She could see Rourke for only another moment through the German helicopter's chin bubble, lost him, and then saw him again, to her left, firing another burst from his assault rifle into the ground as some of the more daring ones with swords began again to advance. She was too close to use her machine guns without risking cutting into the crowd. She flipped the cover back, punched the automatic door-opening button, the fuselage doors opening, Natalia hearing the alarm still, the voice—Icelandic?

She was nearly down, glancing back and left—through the open port-side fuselage door she could see him, running toward the machine, slinging his M-16—he jumped. She heard him shout. "Take her up!"

She hit off PA, onto radio. "This is Natalia—come in Akiro—over."

"Akiro here, Natalia—over!"

"Stand by—out!" And she pushed the radio headset away, shouting back, "John!"

"Paul and Annie—they're here somewhere—keep her low—over toward those buildings on your left," he shouted back. "There's a crowd on the steps there—and I heard gunfire from there before you showed up. Get Akiro down in here—have him position himself over that parkway."

"Right—hang on," and she glanced back once—Rourke held to one of the seat straps with his right fist, his body below the doorframe—he would be standing balanced on the runner, she knew. She banked left, but an easy bank, starting away, the voice beneath them over the loudspeaker still blaring, the alarm still sounding. She shifted her headset into position, speaking into it. "Akiro—into the volcano—stick to the middle—take it slowly—there's a large grassy strip . . ."

There was static. Then Akiro's voice. "Grassy strip in a volcano—please repeat, over."

"I say again—grass strip—affirmative on that—hover over it—keep things confused with the people below. They don't appear to have firearms—but be careful anyway. Natalia out."

She could see the crowd packing the steps of the building far to her left now, the building gray with a darker gray peaked roof, ground-level entrances along the side visible to her, what appeared to be a main entrance at the height of some two dozen steps—a man and woman at the head of the steps. "That's Paul, John—Annie's with him."

"No strafing fire—might ricochet off the concrete of the steps—get in as close as you can and low—I'll jump for it—we'll fight our way out to you."

"Be careful!"

She angled the machine downward, edging laterally now to starboard, no power lines visible, but the tree cover a potential hazard—the altimeter reading was dropping now, dropping—almost to ground level. "I'm jumping clear — now!"

She looked back quickly once — John Rourke was jumping clear.

She could see him in an instant through the chin bubble — he was running toward the steps, his rifle butt impacting a man's face, John jumping to the massive stone-block bannisters flanking the steps, jumping to the next higher level, running, then onto the steps, his assault rifle firing into the air.

Behind her, she could hear Akiro's German helicopter coming into the volcano, and as she looked back, funnel clouds of steam were billowing downward in his wake.

The crowd was edging back, John and Paul and Annie starting to descend the steps, John's assault rifle in his left fist, his Python in his right, Annie with a pistol — perhaps Paul's. But she was pulling back at him, Paul shaking her off.

A voice — the mechanical-sounding voice was gone, some taped warning, she imagined. A new voice. A woman's voice — gentle-sounding. The voice was in English. "Please do not fire. We are peaceful people and mean you no harm. Please do not fire!"

Natalia on impulse hit the PA switch — if she could hear the voice of the woman over the loudspeaker, perhaps the woman could hear her. "Who are you? Why do you hold Annie Rourke prisoner?"

After a moment the loudspeaker voice returned. "She was saved by one of our law enforcement officers when one of the helicopter machines was observed landing. Would you land?"

Natalia looked at John beneath her, still descending the steps. She spoke into her microphone. "Who are you?"

"I am Sigrid Jokli, President of Lydveldid Island — the Republic of Iceland."

Natalia closed her eyes for an instant. Then into the microphone over the PA system, "Tell your people to back away, to return to their homes or wherever—then my leader can speak with you as we speak now."

There was a pause, then the woman's voice again. "Very well," and the woman paused again, then spoke again, but in Icelandic. The crowds on the steps—they began edging right, those nearest the height of the steps with noticeable trepidation passing John and Paul and Annie, starting into the structure.

Natalia switched back to radio. "Akiro—did you hear that? Natalia over."

"This is crazy, Natalia—what do I do? Over."

"If the crowd backs away, land, but keep your engines running, be ready for takeoff—you and Sarah and Michael and Madison, stay inside. I'm landing too. Keep your radio open—out." She swung the helicopter a full 360 degrees—everywhere, the men and women were moving indoors, John and Paul and Annie alone now on the steps of the four-storied structure. John was waving her down—Natalia started to descend.

Chapter Eighteen

Sarah had cut in on the radio—how was Annie?
Natalia had confirmed Annie seemed well, then signed
off and brought the machine fully down, taking her
own advice, leaving the rotors turning as John, Paul,
and Annie backed toward the helicopter, John and Paul
still covering the building steps.

The woman's voice still echoed in Icelandic over the
loudspeaker system, John approaching the machine
now. Natalia moved to the open fuselage door, one of
her revolvers in her right fist. She jumped down,
ducking her head, her hair caught up in the draft from
the rotors, her left hand pushing it back from her face.

Annie—Natalia went to her, hugging the girl, Annie
hugging her. "Are you all right?" Natalia asked loudly
over the hum of the rotors.

"Yes, I'm fine—these people—they're good people,
Natalia."

"Did you—when you stabbed Blackburn—?"

"He didn't—"

"I know that—but the way you did it—I found
myself thinking about what I did years ago once, when
we were down in Argentina—we were taking this
woman and her babies to safety and I started thinking
about once when I was very young—"

"You were with Vladmir, your husband, but he had

you do something and you were captured—you let the man—well—let him think—"

"Shh, child," and Natalia embraced Annie close against her, Natalia's body shivering: the girl's mind—it frightened her.

John Rourke's voice on the PA system. "My name is John Rourke. The girl you had here is my daughter."

"You are welcome here in friendship," the woman's voice returned.

"Madame President," Rourke began again. "What the hell is going on here?"

"Please keep your weapons if you feel more secure with them. I will dispatch three of our law enforcement personnel to accompany you to my residence where all of your questions can be answered. None of you will come to harm."

Natalia felt John's voice hesitate, then, "I'll come alone. The rest of the people with me will remain with our helicopters."

"Please—bring your daughter."

Before Rourke could answer, Annie, Natalia still embracing her called, "Daddy—please?"

John Rourke didn't speak, Annie saying, "Please, Daddy—it'll be all right."

John Rourke's voice. "All right—but we'll both be armed. At the first sign of treachery, this time we will take lives."

Annie, Natalia releasing her, went to the fuselage, calling up to her father, "Tell them I want to go inside and change—please."

Natalia smiled, John Rourke's eyes flashing through bewilderment into anger and then to amusement. "My daughter has asked to be allowed to change from her nightgown."

"The guards will make certain none of you come to harm. Yes—and then come to my residence."

Rourke spoke once more. "Agreed — we'll wait here." He threw down the microphone, jumping down from the fuselage and hugging his daughter to him, Annie's arms circling tight around his neck.

Chapter Nineteen

Annie Rourke pulled the nightgown over her head and called from the bathroom to Natalia. "It's beautiful here, isn't it?"

"Yes—like some Judeo-Christian Garden of Eden— it's amazing."

When the guards had arrived, her father had sent Natalia in with her to guard the door while she changed. She hadn't told him it was unnecessary— besides the fact that she thought he was sweet to be so protective, she welcomed the chance to talk with Natalia, as she always had. "We don't have anything to be afraid of here."

She heard Natalia laugh. "Maybe that's why your father is so skeptical . . ." and Natalia laughed again.

Annie stepped into the panties—lace-trimmed, very delicate looking, loaned to her along with the rest of the clothing, her own clothes having been taken off by some of the women who had brought her these things, to be cleaned, she presumed. There was no bra—none of the women here wore them, having instead high, wide, waist-cinching belts over their dresses or skirts and blouses. She stepped into the ankle-length petti-coat, tying it at her waist. She had found the small apartment she had been given to use quite modern— running water, electricity, shower, a comfortable bed, comfortable chairs, books—all in Icelandic. But the people themselves seemed to resist the modern in their personal habits from what little she had seen of them, from watching their style of dress, the simplicity of their smiles, their manner.

The guard or policeman or whatever he was that Paul had hit on the side of the head had been stretchered away by four men, the man still conscious, her father aiding one of the medics with a pressure bandage.

She pulled the blouse over her head, adjusting the balloon sleeves, closing the tiny buttons at the cuffs. She settled the neckline, tying the low-cut neckline's small blue ribbon bow. It was as if they had never heard of elastic. The fabrics—cotton and wool only. The blouse was cotton, the ankle-length full skirt into which she stepped wool, a bright blue, brighter seeming against the white of the blouse. It buttoned at the side, and as she worked the buttons she heard Natalia call to her from the bedroom, "How do you think these people survived here, Annie?"

"Maybe they had the dome sealed—the dome of the volcano?" She finished buttoning the skirt, picked up the wide leather belt. It was real leather.

"That's possible, I suppose—but then why remove the dome?"

"When the atmosphere got thicker . . ."

"I don't know."

Annie settled the belt, then laced it at the front across her abdomen, tying the lacings into a bow. Her hair—she liked the way the girls here braided theirs, then put it up, but there was no time to experiment. She used the brush—one of her own things from her coat pocket—and started to work her hair. "Why do you think it is that they carry swords instead of guns?" She continued brushing her hair, walking from the bathroom into the bedroom, Natalia perched on the edge of the bed.

"You look pretty—Paul will go crazy over you," Natalia laughed.

Annie twirled once around, the skirt ballooning around her legs, laughed. "Yeah—he will, won't he?"

"I don't know—guns seem alien to them—but they seem familiar with what guns are. Very strange!"

"Hmm—Michael and Madison—are they all right?"

Natalia nodded. "I wish I still smoked. No—when I signaled Akiro, I told Sarah to have Michael and Madison come with her. There's nothing at the little base camp we established except the Russian helicopter Blackburn used. Sarah told me they emptied it of fuel once Akiro arrived, and the weapons systems equipment isn't interchangeable. We can fire a missile into it as we leave. But Michael and Madison are fine. Your mother's pregnant—at least she thinks she is. Women are supposed to be able to tell by something in the eyes, I always heard. Well, if it's true, I see it in your mother's eyes."

"Momma—a baby?"

"I think, anyway. That's none of my business."

"I wish . . ."

Natalia stood up, Annie pulling her own shawl across her shoulders, the one item of her clothing that hadn't been taken off for cleaning or whatever. Natalia smiled. "I read some rhyme once—about if wishes were fishes. Well—I can't remember the rest. Come on—you and your father have to meet Madame President." Natalia started for the door.

Annie whispered, "Wait. What will you do? I mean—if Momma is pregnant—then Daddy could—"

"Could never—I know that. But I've known that all along. It was doomed from the start. When this is all over," and Natalia smiled, but a sad smile, a lonely smile, "I mean, when we've finally defeated Vladmir's forces—well. There should be plenty to do. I'm pretty good at electronics, with computers. I can find something useful to do . . ."

"But I mean—"

Natalia lowered her head, lowered her voice—Annie wanted to hold her, make Natalia's hurt go away. Natalia said, "I was married once. I fell in love once. Not with the same man. When the man I married is finally dead, and the world and everyone in it is safe from his evil, then I'll leave the man I fell in love with. That's all," and Natalia opened the door and passed through the doorway into the corridor. Annie Rourke shut off the bedroom light and followed her outside.

Chapter Twenty

John Rourke held his daughter's right hand in his left. With the way she had been dressed when she reemerged from the building, to have given her a pistol belt would have been ludicrous, and for her to carry a gun in her hand would have been awkward. He had told her, "If there's trouble, take my pistol belt and the Python and run for the nearest helicopter. Don't worry about me because I'll be right behind you."

"Okay," she had smiled, and leaned up on her tiptoes and kissed him on the lips lightly. He had watched her as she had kissed Paul—hard. John Rourke anticipated that once Annie and Paul got the opportunity, he would be well on his way toward potential grandfatherhood for the second time.

He was hardly in a position to insist on a church wedding—even if there had been a church. The concept of marriage being in the heart and mind rather than printed on a marriage certificate was something he had always believed in. In heart and mind, Paul and his daughter were already married, as were Michael and gentle little Madison.

He had placed a hand on each of their shoulders—Paul's and Annie's—saying, "Hey guys—I love you both."

Paul had smiled, holding Annie tighter.

Against Paul's protests that she shouldn't go, they

had gone, Annie telling him not to worry and leaving it at that. As they walked now, the three green-clad, sword-carrying law enforcement officers ahead of them, Annie whispered, "You mean what I think you meant?"

"It depends on what you think I meant."

"I mean—the 'hey guys' part—you mean—"

"I don't know—you and Paul—"

"Well—we want to—we were waiting for Commander Dodd to marry us."

"You'd be better off having nobody say words over you than having that asshole do it."

"All right. You know—I think Paul figures because I'm your daughter—"

"I know that. Let him know he'll still be my best friend even when he's my son-in-law."

"This is crazy."

"What's crazy?—I mean, in particular."

She laughed. "I mean—How old are you?"

"Old enough," he laughed.

She let loose of his hand and hugged his left arm with both her arms, Rourke feeling himself smile. "Five hundred and—"

"Ohh, shut up—but okay, you're this side of forty. I'm gonna be twenty-eight in a couple of weeks."

"Try closer to a week and a half."

"And Momma?"

"Closer to thirty than forty. Remember? I aged five years that she didn't when I played games with the cryogenic chambers."

Annie cleared her throat, Rourke looking at her for an instant—she almost seemed to be blushing. They were walking along what literally was a garden path, behind the three guards. He hoped it wouldn't prove the figurative garden path. "What do you want to ask me?"

"Well—ahh—Natalia—she, ahh—she said she thought maybe Momma was—"

"Pregnant?"

"Uh-huh."

"Too early to tell—as a physician. But as the man who did it, I'd say there's a substantial possibility the assumption was correct."

"Ohh, wow."

"Hoping for a little baby brother or baby sister?"

"Ohh, Daddy—I mean that's great for you guys."

"Why? Because it'll keep us together? We would have stayed together anyway."

"Well—I know that, but—" She hugged his arm more tightly now. "What are you going to do about—ahh—about Natalia?"

Rourke didn't look at his daughter. "I don't know. I can't be unfaithful to your mother—at least not in fact. I don't know. Wish to God I did—now change the subject or be quiet."

Her grip on his arm relaxed an instant, then resumed its tightness—Rourke focused his concentration on the three guards, on the questions he would ask the woman who called herself the President of Iceland, on the wisdom of leaving his M-16 with Paul and Natalia at the helicopter—on anything but Annie's question . . .

It was the building at the far end of the grassy strip from which Natalia had plucked him with the helicopter, the rather imposing, official-seeming building.

They began mounting the steps. His watch showed nearly two in the morning—perhaps not Icelandic time. But the lavender grow lights made everything bright as day.

The plants grew twenty-four hours a day here, produced oxygen, used up carbon dioxide.

The steps were low, more for decoration than for

getting someplace, and at the head of the steps he saw a woman. Was it Sigrid Jokli? he wondered. Madame President?

She was dressed similarly to Annie—peasant blouse, ankle-length print skirt, a shawl about her shoulders. No jewelry that he could detect from the distance. Her age seemed indeterminate. She was at least his age, perhaps older, perhaps quite a bit older. Her pale blond hair was braided, the braids entwined at the crown of her head, themselves forming something like a crown. He wondered absently if such a hairstyle were perhaps at the origin of the old phrase about hair being a woman's crowning glory. Etymology had always fascinated him, but not to the point where he had pursued the discipline to any great degree.

She had a pretty face—the kind of face that men came home to, the smile warm seeming if a bit reserved. Under the circumstances, with armed invaders ascending her Capitol Building, which he assumed this to be, he couldn't blame her.

As they ascended, nearing the height of the steps now, he could see her eyes—green, pretty.

She started down the steps, the fingers of her left hand touching at the fabric of her skirt, raising it, her right hand extending toward him. Rourke stopped as she stopped, clasping her hand. "I am Sigrid Jokli."

"I'm Dr. John Rourke."

"A doctor? Of what discipline?"

"Medicine, ma'am."

"And this girl—she is your daughter?" The voice was soft—a melodic soprano. "But you are too young, sir."

"It's a long story—but I'm more concerned with hearing your story first. I understand one of your policemen saved my daughter's life. I'd like to have the opportunity to meet the gentleman so I may personally thank him."

"Certainly—Bjorn will be called for."

"No need to awaken him," Rourke smiled.

"Our law enforcement personnel have not slept since the alarm was sounded."

"Let me apologize—and I realize that in itself is inadequate. But we've undergone some trying times recently and I was concerned that my daughter might come to some harm here."

"We have all undergone trying times, Dr. Rourke—please. Although the hour is somewhat bizarre, would you and your lovely daughter take refreshment with me?"

"Thank you," Rourke said. She seemed very nice, honey-coated at the edges, the eyes warm-seeming and alert. But he had no intention of consuming anything here until he first had some answers.

She offered her arm, Rourke taking it, his hand to her elbow, Annie still on his left side as they ascended the rest of the steps . . .

The interior of the building—she had explained it was analogous to the White House, both residence and office—was simple, almost to the point of being spartan. But it was a style of decorating he had always liked, the Scandinavian style which this at least emulated, perhaps perpetuated.

They had passed through a long entry hall, the three policemen passing through the wide doorway behind them, a woman who was apparently a housekeeper holding the door on the left, the right-side door remaining closed. Sigrid Jokli had spoken in Icelandic and the three guards had fallen off, Madame Jokli leading them along the hall, stopping before a second set of double doors, sliding them apart into the walls, then passing through the doorway. Rourke kept Annie beside him as he passed through after Madame Jokli.

The room seemed at once library, conference room,

and den. There was a hearth, massive, of flagstone like that used in the path, but the hearth was still and the logs inside it on the brightly polished brass andirons seemed more for appearance than for heat. About the hearth in a pleasantly disorganized manner were placed chairs, the frames of polished and rubbed wood, the wood gleaming, atop the wooden frames comfortable cushions. Beside each chair was a matching footstool.

Books lined the walls, the walls reaching some twelve feet high, he judged. Ladders were spaced along various sections of the shelves. The portions of the walls that were not covered with bookcases were darkly, richly paneled. It was a man's room, and Madame Jokli, so feminine-looking, sounding, acting, seemed somehow at once both out of place and perfectly at home.

A conference table, spartan-seeming, straight-back wooden chairs on all sides, dominated the far end of the massive room toward the forward section of the residence.

"Please — sit down, be comfortable. The young lady's name is Annie?" And she smiled.

"Yes ma'am," Annie told her, perching on the edge of one of the chairs, folding her hands in her lap.

Rourke waited for Madame Jokli to be seated, then took a third chair, leaning back into it. It was comfortable — in the extreme, he thought.

Annie removed her shawl, folded it, set it over the arm of the chair, then replaced her hands in her lap. Madame Jokli spoke. "I understand your motivation in coming here. I called you to speak with me because you are the first visitors from the outside world — which we had thought ceased to exist — since the great fires of five centuries ago. If there are people such as yourselves in the world today, we wish to know."

"You have no weapons—beyond swords," Annie said suddenly. "I'm sorry—I was just kinda curious."

"A good question," Rourke nodded, approving.

Madame Jokli nodded, her smile vanishing. "We saw no need for weapons. The swords our law enforcement personnel carry are carried as a badge of office, much like the green uniforms they wear." Rourke turned quickly toward the still-opened door—a small dog, a puppy.

Rourke looked at Madame Jokli. "You have—"

"Dogs," she smiled. "Cats. No rats—we eliminated them centuries ago. We have some few horses in the hope that someday the climate will warm to the point where they could be extensively bred. They would be useful transportation"—she smiled again—"and besides, they are so pretty, I think. We have domestic livestock—a source of meat protein, milk, wool, leather. We love cheeses here—I could have a cheese board prepared!"

"Ahh—a bit early in the morning for me, ma'am—thank you."

"I like cheese," Annie chimed in.

At that moment the housekeeper who had held the door—white hair done in a bun at the nape of her neck, a dark gray dress, long white apron, her back slightly bent, shoulders slightly stooped—entered to just inside the doorway. She addressed Madame Jokli in Icelandic, the two conversing for a moment, the woman curtseying, leaving, drawing the doors closed behind her.

"I asked for coffee for you, Dr. Rourke—you look like a man who enjoys coffee. I'm having coffee as well, though I prefer tea. But I assumed you perhaps wouldn't drink something that I wasn't drinking—although I seem to remember from some of the old novels of espionage and high adventure I read as a girl

145

that sometimes coffee cups or glasses for alcoholic beverages could themselves be coated with some poison . . ." She shrugged, smiled, then looked at Annie. "And I ordered cheese for you, and hot chocolate—I hope you'll enjoy it."

Annie looked at Rourke, then at the woman. "Thank you very much, ma'am."

"May I ask concerning your English, ma'am?" Rourke began.

"Yes. Before I became President of our little republic, I worked as a scientist, and although my presidential duties take me away from my first professional love, I still ply my trade, so to speak. Among the scientific community, English is quite common simply because so much of the scientific literature is written in the language and translation is sometimes so subjective. We have videotapes of English language films and audio cassettes that are used with our language classes. I must confess, I developed a fine taste for American westerns of five centuries ago, but I had to switch to detective stories because I was using 'ain't' all the time when I spoke your language. Aside from Icelandic, most members of our scientific community speak at least two other languages, from among English, as I indicated, and German, French, Russian, and Japanese."

"Akiro should be pleased."

"A Japanese, Annie?"

"Yes, ma'am—he was a Japanese naval lieutenant."

"Ahh—he can help us if he will. The writings of Tokugawa—"

"The physicist?"

"Yes, Dr. Rourke. You are conversant with the science of five centuries ago?"

"Only modestly," Rourke smiled. "You've explained the languages—but your very existence? You constantly allude to five centuries ago . . ."

"Yes," she smiled. "Don't I? If you are conversant with the science of the pre-Conflagration epoch, then you must be aware of the fact that Iceland was a world leader in the use of geothermal energy, as was Japan by the way."

Rourke only nodded, wanting a cigar, but not impolite enough to light one.

"At any event," she continued, arranging her skirt, refolding her hands in her lap, "some scientific researchers gradually came up with the idea of utilizing a verifiably dormant volcano as a massive geothermal-powered, environment-controlled garden. Previously, we had utilized conventional greenhouses heated with hot water pumped from geothermal wells. Much of our conventional heating for buildings and dwellings utilized this resource. The thing to do of course was come up with the proper volcano. That took several years and detailed studies. At the time, there were approximately two hundred volcanoes of varying size in the country. Eventually, Hekla was settled upon because of size and dormancy. The project was not kept particularly secret, but there were some proprietary processes involved that there was apparently some concern over—regarding the processes being copied, as the story goes. So, no announcements were made of the program. It was simply begun with the able volunteer assistance of university students and even some private individuals who had helped finance the project. It was a hands-on affair. It took many years. It was all but complete when the war between the United States and her allies and the Union of Soviet Socialist Republics broke out. Some wise men—and women too, I hope"—she smiled—"took it upon themselves to alter the original plan. Livestock, medical supplies, persons even brought their dogs and cats, the ancestors of those you will see about our land here. Approximately two hundred people moved here to work and to prepare in the event that environmental catastrophe should result from the war—as it did. Many more moved in as the situation worsened around the world."

"But how did you survive?" Annie began. "The sky— I was a little girl when it happened, but I watched on the television monitors Daddy had—"

The woman's hands shook. "You were a little . . ."

Rourke licked his lips. "I told you—a complicated story."

"But that is impossible," Madame Jokli said softly. "Human beings cannot live—it—it's—"

"It is at once impossible and yet perfectly explainable," Rourke smiled. "Cryogenic sleep chambers developed by NASA—the United States National Aeronautics and Space Administration—for use in deep space travel, coupled with a special cryogenic serum which allowed the reawakening of the subject by preventing a type of brain death. I was born in the middle of the twentieth century, as were the others with me with one exception: the wife of my son, Michael— you'll meet her. She is perhaps the last survivor of a survival community that subsisted beneath the surface for five centuries. Her name is Madison."

"Those lights in the sky—the high altitude—"

"It was called the Eden Project, ma'am—originally one hundred twenty persons of all races and from all free nations. A preparation for doomsday. You are not alone on the earth."

"But we had thought—" The doors opened, Rourke looking toward them quickly. The white-haired old woman entered, pushing a teacart, then closed the doors behind her and pushed the teacart along the polished wooden floors. Madame Jokli spoke with her and the woman curtseyed and started away, reopening, reclosing the doors. Madame Jokli said, "I told her I would serve."

"Ohh—can I?" Annie asked.

"Yes—certainly, my dear," Madame Jokli smiled. She leaned back in her chair—rather heavily, Rourke thought. Annie poured the coffee—Rourke didn't know if Annie genuinely wanted to play tea party at her age or simply wanted to make sure her father didn't get a mickeyed cup of coffee. There was also the gambit of poisoning both cups, or entirely poisoning the contents of the pot and the person doing the poisoning prearranging to take the antidote—and then calmly poisoning himself—or herself.

Rourke took the cup from Annie. There was what looked like fresh cream and sugar. Madame Jokli used the cream, Annie pouring for her. Rourke decided that Annie really had wanted to play tea party. Lastly she poured herself hot chocolate, the smell of the fresh cocoa almost overpowering. She passed around small plates, Rourke taking one just to be pleasant. Annie sat beside him again, studying his face. He shrugged—he sipped at his coffee, smelling it as he brought it to his lips. It smelled like coffee. To be doubly certain, he asked Annie to pour a bit of the cream into it. The cream tasted and smelled like cream—it was cold and fresh.

"How did you survive here?" Rourke asked the woman again.

She sipped at her coffee, Annie nibbling at a piece of cheese. "Through force of will and God's Providence we were spared—His Providence allowed us to plan ahead, and the combined wills of our people allowed us to meet the hardships and not only subsist, but thrive. Our scientists have since discovered that a bizarre variation in the magnetosphere combined with an anomalous relationship between the Van Allen radia-

149

tion belts and the aurora apparently constructed what was, in essence, a particle shield preventing the normal process of atmospheric mixing. What destroyed your earth saved ours. I'm not a physicist, but rather a biologist, our most common discipline here. But should you care for a more accurate and detailed explanation, I can arrange for you to meet with specific members of our scientific community and they can offer their interpretations. Suffice it to say, we almost literally watched as the sky took flame. Rings of flame surrounded us here for days, as the accounts go. There was nothing to do but pray, to spend the last moments with loved ones, to weep for those beyond the pale of our land."

"All of Iceland?"

"Yes. Iceland was spared. But with the burning of the skies and the planet shift—there was one, I'm sure you know—the cold gripped our land as never before. This was the time of greatest sorrow. There was famine; nothing that ran by fossil fuels which had been imported prior to your war could run now. No food products could be wasted in the production of ethyl alcohol. The community here strove to produce as much food as the land would allow, because this was the only available land. A man rose among our people—he was known only as Pjetur. The people listened to him." Her eyes were filling with tears. "He preached a gospel of what was called 'scientific survival'—that only the most fit should be allowed to live, those who were too well advanced in age or physically or mentally afflicted should be euthanized. Our church spoke out against it. So did our scientists. There was revolution, begun by Pjetur. There was civil war. Our home here became a citadel, a safe haven for those who believed that the philosophy of Pjetur was anathema. And there was a final battle. By that time, our population of some quarter million had been thrice decimated, and when that last major battle was over Pjetur's forces were defeated. Some hundred thousand of us were alive two decades later. The birth rate was voluntarily reduced. Within fifty years, the food shortages, the hardships, the reduced birthrate, had lessened our population to some fifty thousand. The standard of living was slightly upgraded, but still there was not enough food and there was voluntary rationing. There was voluntary birth control. Within fifty more years, our population was twenty-five thousand. Still, there could be no means to make the land beyond this volcano and some few others workable. A great conference of scientific, religious, and political leaders was held—here. It was determined that the land beyond the pale of the volcanoes would be abandoned. It was called the Migration of Sorrow. Our people went to the volcanoes. Hekla is the capitol. There are five other city-states, all of them smaller. In this building, our parliament meets four times a year. Travel beyond the volcanoes is arduous, so rather than a parliament of older men and women, the Althing, as it is called and has been called, of necessity is young. Perhaps our ideas are young too. I am fifty-three—old for someone in government."

You look marvelously young," Rourke told her truthfully. "And very beautiful, ma'am."

Sigrid Jokli smiled.

Chapter Twenty-one

There were two bands of personnel from Hekla who regularly left the warmth of paradise for the cold of the glaciers and the snowfields — the law enforcement and the miners. Mining was an intermittent occupation, only done for the raw materials for steel-making, itself an intermittent occupation, a cottage industry. What was built, was built of granite blocks, and with voluntary population control, there was never a need for additional housing. The cottage industry, practiced by those same persons who mined, was the fabrication of edged weapons, for ceremonial use, for decoration, for beauty. These same persons fabricated laboratory equipment for research.

Word from the German forces under Captain Hartman established their arrival at two hours, by six in the evening. Rourke and the others of his party — in shifts, for precaution — had each slept six hours, bathed, eaten, and generally refreshed themselves. Annie had found young women her own age from among the scientists who spoke English and were eager for the opportunity to practice. Natalia, because of her native fluency in Russian and her extensive technical education, became a hub of interest among many of the older members of the scientific corps, especially the men. Akiro Kurinami too had found great popularity, and was already at work aiding in deciphering the fine nuances of meaning in the works of the physicist Tokugawa. The arrival of the Germans under Captain Hartman was eagerly awaited in the hopes of initiating an exchange of technological data.

Rourke had not considered the Eden Project as being the salvation of future civilization, but these people, and curiously the Germans, did. Both cultures had survived much, taken divergent paths, and at last found a system of freedom, albeit the Germans had not found peace. Colonel Mann under express orders from Dieter Bern was to aid in prosecution of the war against Karamatsov and the Soviet forces, in the hopes of ending war once and for all.

Of the latter hope, John Rourke entertained little hope for success—but he would work toward ending war as any sane man would, regardless of the prospects.

Paul Rubenstein had found himself swamped by the leaders of the state-supported Evangelical Lutheran Church—Judaism was unknown here. Perhaps most heartening here, Rourke found, was the eagerness to know, to understand, to acquire knowledge for the sake of knowledge. There was work done in aerodynamics, yet these people used no automobiles, no aircraft.

Sarah had found a niche as well. Painting and artwork of any kind was almost reverentially treated here, and Sarah's career as artist and illustrator had involved her with the University by the time they had breakfasted at noon, Sigrid Jokli eliciting their backgrounds in a manner that seemed to be driven more by curiosity and innocence than by reasons of prying or information gathering.

Madison and Michael were the focus of attention of the historians—Madison for the history of the culture from which she had sprung, Michael for his remembrances of the aftermath of The Night of The War and his experiences since awakening from the cryogenic sleep; but the real focus of interest was Madison.

Elaine Halversen's scientific specialties had drawn great interest from the scientific community, but even more interest was generated by her chocolate brown skin. None of the people here had ever seen a black person and had happily greeted the news that more were with the Eden Project survivors.

Rourke had spent several hours in conversation with Madame Jokli and others — recalling the events leading to The Night of The War, the events since — and he had excused himself to walk about the place alone. Bitter memories, dead friends. He often found himself thinking of the heroic General Varakov — a soldier, a patriot to his native Russia, but above all a human being capable of great insight and feeling, but, like all the rest, dead.

When he had excused himself, Madame Jokli had told him to visit the house of Jon, the last name escaping him as unpronounceable. But aside from their similarity of first names they would find commonality of interest. In his late sixties, Jon had retired from his work in science and devoted his time to the crafting of edged weapons, always a hobby, a skill learned from his father who had been one of those who ventured forth into the cold to mine metal for ornate swords, for scientific equipment. Jon himself did not venture into the cold anymore, but rather his son, a biologist, did it for him.

But Jon spoke English because of his scientific background.

There was no telephone system — it had never been found necessary. Radios linked one community to another, volcano to volcano, but beyond that all communication was written or by word of mouth. Jon would know that Rourke was coming. Rourke had agreed to go.

The walk along the creatively but logically laid out garden pathways was pleasant and peaceful, the pretty girls in their long dresses nodding, smiling, some of them giggling, the older persons watching from porches or balconies, waving or sometimes only watching.

People here lived in a mixture of private family inherited residences or larger apartment complexes.

It was much like a twentieth-century city, but without the problems of cities of that era, and set amid a pollution-free, climate-controlled garden.

He could never live like this—nothing changed, he had realized early.

He followed the house numbers—some houses had no numbers or the numbers were obscured by vines or climbing plants. Everyone knew everyone and where everyone lived. He had noticed too that there were no locks. But those house numbers visible had led him to a two-story house, the same pyramidal roof structure, unnecessary here but a remnant from the architecture of the outside where roofs had to be built to withstand the weight of heavy snows and to shed the snows at the first melting.

A low, narrow porch fronted the door and Rourke took the steps and knocked.

The door opened after a moment. A tall man, his body beneath the gray long-sleeved shirt seeming muscular and vastly younger than the flowing mane of white hair and the white beard contrarily indicated. He wore loose-fitting darker gray slacks, wrinkled at the bottoms from being stuffed into boot tops as Rourke had noticed was the custom here. But he wore no boots, but rather slippers of soft-looking leather.

"I'm—"

"I know who you are—welcome!" The man extended his right hand. Rourke took it, the man clasping his left hand over Rourke's right. "I am honored, sir—come in, please!"

"You're sure I'm not disturbing you?"

"Disturbing me—that is rich indeed! Come!" And he almost dragged Rourke through the doorway. The man's grip was that of a man half his age, his eyes clear, alight with interest, blue like all the other eyes here. The house was modest, utilitarian, comfortable seeming, the walls white like the exterior of the house, the windows opening outward toward the garden walkway in front. The man clapped his hands together in glee, Rourke noticed as the man eyed his weapons, Rourke's eyes scanning the paintings, the swords, the first firearms he had seen here—an engraved, ivory-gripped percussion revolver and a Kentucky-style flintlock rifle. "I am the only man here who has guns. They have been passed down for generations. No one uses them," he laughed, "and no powder is available with which to fire them, but they are family heirlooms. Please—while I get some refreshments—please . . ." and he gestured toward the wall where the two guns and several of the swords and a painting in the style of Van Gogh, but not a Van Gogh, hung.

"I'm putting you to too much trouble, sir. . . "

"Nonsense—we heard you would come—we hoped you would come. My wife has been baking pastries—please?"

The man scratched his head, his face etched momentarily with puzzlement, and then lit with a smile. "The forest telegraph!"

"Jungle telegraph," Rourke smiled.

"Yes—please," and Jon left the room, disappearing toward the rear of the house.

Rourke approached the wall with the two guns. The

percussion revolver was a Colt Third Model Dragoon, the type Wild Bill Hickok had favored over all others. It looked original, rather than one of the new-edition Colt blackpowder guns introduced in the 1970s, but Rourke could not be sure. The quality of the Colt new editions had been such that some skillful and unscrupulous persons had been able to disguise them to appear as originals, so well disguised that at times experienced collectors were hard tested to know the difference. Rourke did not count himself this knowledgeable. But it was beautiful.

The flintlock rifle was—"You are a doctor—yes?"

Rourke turned away from the rifle—Jon had reentered, a plump, chubby-faced, white-haired woman carrying a tray with him. Something smelled good. "Yes—a doctor of medicine. And I understand you are a biochemist."

"Yes—yes," and he gestured dismissively with his hands.

The woman set down the tray, smiled, curtseyed, and started to leave.

"My wife—she speaks no English, cares nothing for weapons—but she is a fine woman. Anyway, the last thing she needs to do is eat—please—sit yourself."

"Thank you," Rourke smiled, seating himself on a light-colored Scandinavian-type couch with square leather cushions.

"Are those original?" and Rourke gestured to the wall.

"Yes—the guns belonged to my ancestor who first settled here. It has required constant attention over the years to keep them in perfect condition as they are—the humidity here, you know."

"Excellent—I can see why you are so proud of them. And the swords?"

Jon smiled as he sat down. "Please," and gestured to

the coffee, the pastries, which were round and covered in sugar. "I have contributed one sword to that wall, as did my father, and his father before him. And so on," and he smiled. "It is a very good thing it is a large and sturdy wall."

The coffee was good to drink, the pastries richer than Rourke was at all used to or had ever favored, but good—plums and apple pieces inside each pastry. Rourke learned they were of Danish origin and were called *Aebleskivers*.

They spoke of sword-making, knife-making, of the community inside Hekla, of the other communities that formed Iceland as it was today. "Weapons are for decoration only. Those men you fought when you entered here—and those men who were willing to fight you—they have never before raised a sword in battle. It is a ceremonial tradition. You see, once our society was formed, weapons were the last thing anyone wanted here. Warfare had brought about the destruction of the rest of the earth, we had thought, and the internecine warfare here in Iceland had nearly destroyed us. No laws were suggested prohibiting weapons, no need really, there was a general dislike for their use. But early on, it was determined that for order, law enforcement would be needed, and that some type of weapon might from time to time be required. Hence the swords—we have always been traditionally-minded here in Iceland, and mindful too of our Viking heritage. Hence, the sword seemed perfect. In the early days there was occasionally crime. Now there is not—we have removed all necessity, real or imagined, for criminal activity. We have made tremendous strides against mental illness. Combining both factors, crime is unknown. But the sword has become a symbol— oddly, for peace, here—and it alone has guarded us for five centuries. Not since the earliest days here has one been used to let blood."

"I'm sorry if we've brought violence back to you."

"Life is many things — our lives here are restricted. Restricted in the sense that we have limited experiences of the world, because we have our own world only. The young men who enter law enforcement practice with their swords, never expecting to use them. Perhaps you will have caused them to take their practice more seriously," Jon laughed. "Your guns — may I see them?"

"Certainly," he nodded. He carried only the twin stainless Detonics Combat Master .45s, the Python locked away in the helicopters, as were the other weapons. He withdrew one of the pistols with his right hand, snapping it from the Alessi rig. He pushed the magazine-release catch, then worked back the slide, his left palm over the ejection port to catch the chambered round. He visibly inspected the open chamber, let the slide run forward, and lowered the hammer, then handed the pistol to Jon. Had the man been a twentieth-century man with so avid an interest in weapons, Rourke might have handed over the pistol with the slide locked back. But he doubted Jon would understand the operation of the pistol.

"And this is?"

"A Detonics Combat Master, in .45 ACP."

"ACP?"

"It originally stood for Automatic Colt Pistol."

"Ahh — and the metal? It seems of excellent quality."

"A variety of stainless steels. Early stainless-steel semi-automatic handguns had problems with lubricating and were prone to galling. Detonics conquered the problem with their guns and others followed suit. It's basically a Colt-Browning design, a single-action as you can see, in that respect like the Third Model Dragoon you have on the wall. But of course the gas expended during firing works to operate the slide, and

159

each time the slide moves rearward a spent round is ejected and a fresh one chambered from the magazine as it goes forward." Rourke held up the six-round magazine for the pistol, which he had removed to safe it. "—Until the magazine runs out," he added. He inserted the loose round under the feed lips. "I use 185-grain jacketed hollow points—at least until I run out."

"You live by this—this and the other one in your case?"

"A holster—but no. I live with them as aids. I live by what I feel is right. These are tools, much like the tools you used in your laboratory when you were a scientist."

"Why does a healer use weapons?"

Rourke took one of his cigars from his pocket—the older man was lighting a pipe. "May I?"

"Yes, certainly." Rourke lit the cigar in the blue-yellow flame of his battered Zippo. "But my question—why?"

Rourke exhaled a thin stream of gray smoke, the smoke hanging in a cloud for an instant, then dissipating through the open windows leading to the path. "I, ahh—I was always interested in firearms, enjoyed shooting as a hobby, was good with guns. I always wanted to be a doctor. I guess I wanted to help people—if that sounds trite, I apologize."

"No—not at all," and Jon fell silent.

"I came to the realization that people seemed dead-set on destruction, on perpetrating all sorts of evil—that working as a doctor was patching up the evil, in essence, not really doing anything to counteract it—at least not as a physician, not for me. I joined my country's intelligence service and worked within that sphere for a number of years, trying to stem the tide of communism and international terrorism. How much good I did, I don't know. Then at last I hit on what I felt could be truly useful, beneficial: Teaching people how to stay alive. I'd always considered life supremely important, that each individual was unique, irreplaceable. I began teaching the knowledge and experience I had gained with weapons, survivalism, the practical applications of medicine for the individual. I wrote about the subjects extensively, conducted seminars, trained a wide range of personnel, both in the classroom context and in the field. But I learned early on that, perhaps because life is so precious, there's always someone who wants to take it, destroy it. My firearms, my edged weapons—like the mind, I use them as a means of preserving life, my loved ones' lives, the lives of people who can't or won't preserve their own. It was fashionably noble at times throughout history to be pacifistic, to vow never to lift a hand against one's fellow man. But life shouldn't be thrown away. I won't throw away mine. I've risked it, would risk it again. Not to defend oneself if the means are even marginally available is suicide, and suicide is, under most circumstances, the total abdication of logic and reason. So, preserving life and the lives of others is of course the ultimate logical act, at least to me. My guns help me with this. Nothing more."

"You are a complex man—and I think you are a hero. We could have been heavily armed, Dr. Rourke, yet you entered here to save your daughter."

"Paul Rubenstein did the same thing. There's nothing extraordinary about that."

"Perhaps—perhaps not. Why did you not kill those guards, or kill there in the park that faces the residence of Madame Jokli?"

"There didn't seem to be a reason for it."

"But surely your guns were superior to our swords."

"Had there been a reason to kill, rest assured I would have."

Jon nodded thoughtfully, handing Rourke back the

161

little Detonics pistol. Rourke put the magazine up the butt, worked the slide, chambering a round, then slowly lowered the hammer over the chambered round, rolling his thumb from between the hammer and the rear face of the slide for added safety.

"I will show you my work — come."

Rourke nodded, stood as Jon stood, then followed the older man down the length of the sitting room and into a narrow hallway, to a door, then through the doorway. A workshop, attached to the house, primitive by twentieth-century standards. No machinery, but a workshop nonetheless. Windows — closed here — would have opened onto a foundry just outside the house. Along the near wall were wooden pegs, hung into the pegs leather thongs, and suspended from the thongs an array of edged weapons of all sizes and types — swords, fighting knives, hunting knives, skinners, daggers.

"The temptation, of course, since we are a society essentially without violence, would be to use materials that lent themselves better to decoration and were not sturdy enough for actual use. But our guild has rejected this almost as one. Each sword, each knife, is as strong as such an implement can be made, our steels made to the most exacting formula."

"A question?" Rourke began, studying a sword that was not yet completed — the area where the guard and the handle would be was unfinished — merely the finished blade and the full-length tang. "When I followed my daughter here through the snow, I saw the impression of something like a staff in the snow."

Jon laughed. "Bjorn — you followed Bjorn. Bjorn Rolvaag is the one who found your daughter . . ."

"I want to meet him and thank him."

"Yes," the old man nodded. "Bjorn is, as you described yourself, someone interested in survivalism. He spends much time in the snows, enjoys the rugged life. I made his staff for him. He would not mind my showing you—I made two. One for myself." And he walked across the room to a closet, opened the door. Beyond Jon were billets of steel, a wall lined with files. He closed the door, turning around—in his hands was a six-foot length of what looked like stainless steel. As Rourke drew nearer, he could see that hairline-thin joints were spaced every foot or so. The base of the staff was a triangular-shaped spike, the head of the staff a massive knob, also of stainless steel. Jon walked over to one of the workbenches, set the staff down, and began to dismantle it. "It is made of one-and-one-half-inch steel tubing, but the tubing begins as solid bar stock and is machined into the tubular conformation. There are six separate foot-long segments, as you can see." He unscrewed the staff at the center. "I have threaded each segment for the length of three inches. In a single segment, only six inches are unsupported. This will not break. Bjorn, when he helped me to design it, took his staff and used it to pry a boulder weighing more than five hundred pounds. The boulder moved, the staff did not even dent, nor did it bend. The staff is empty, but as you can see, the possibilities for carrying one's need in the staff are endless. A true implement for survival, as well as a formidable weapon, I should think."

"Yes—you're a fine craftsman, sir."

"Thank you, Dr. Rourke. I try to do my best."

"The cave where they apparently rested and warmed themselves—in the cave I found a fire, the fire fueled with bricks of fuel."

Jon smiled. "Yes. These were developed more than a century ago and have never needed improvement. A combination of chemicals, which are safe to store, yet can be lit almost immediately. It was realized that someday our beautiful world here might cease. That someday the geothermal wells which are our life's blood might well become exhausted. For that day, much work has been done. Fortunately, that day has not yet come. We pray it never will come. But the fire bricks, the fabrics from which our outerwear—such as what Bjorn must have worn and such as the miners wear, and those who must travel here for meeting of the Althing—they are designed for survival in extreme cold. The very best."

"When the Germans arrive—I assume you have heard?"

"Yes—I look forward to meeting with them, as we all do. There will be so much to share."

"Yes," Rourke agreed.

The old gentleman lovingly showed Rourke the fine points of each blade, each tool he used to craft his edged weapons by hand. He examined Rourke's little Sting IA Black Chrome, gave it his approval. He had never seen a production knife before. Rourke told him that one of the women—Natalia—carried a unique folding knife and promised to have Natalia drop off to see him and show it to him.

After several hours with the man, Rourke left, walking alone again, along the garden pathways, the clouds of steam above him at the mouth of the crater like clouds against a dark blue sky.

Paradise was here—if one was the sort of person to like paradise. John Rourke wasn't that sort.

Chapter Twenty-two

Michael Rourke had left the university building and walked, the eyes of men and women focusing on him—not on his face, he knew, but on the two .44 Magnum Smith revolvers he carried. His father had been right about the Ruger single-actions—superlative was an inferior word to describe their performance, but they had never been designed for combat use. They weren't fast enough. But he would always be a revolver man, hence had gone to the six-inch Model 629 and the four-inch, identical except for barrel lengths.

The people here were friendly, considerate, concerned, intelligent, and it gave him the creeps. Walking was easier now, the German miracle spray, whatever it was, having promoted recovery to such an extent that his surgery was almost healed.

He didn't quite feel himself ready to practice his martial arts katas yet, but he could walk, move about, do things generally with reasonable normalcy.

He walked along one of the garden paths, a fruit orchard to his left, the fruit forced, in various stages from budding flower to ripe fruit ready to be picked.

"Hey—Michael!"

He looked behind him, stopped—it was Paul Rubenstein. He waved back to Paul and waited. "They through grilling you on Judaism?" he laughed good-naturedly.

"Yeah — I see they've still got Madison, huh?"

"And Annie?"

"Yeah," Paul laughed.

"Goin' for a walk. Wanna join me?"

"Sure," and Paul Rubenstein fell in beside him. The eyes stared doubly now as they walked, conversing about the people here, the eyes not only on Michael's Smith & Wesson but on Paul's shoulder holster with the battered-looking Browning High Power in it. "I see you've switched off the Rugers."

"A Super Blackhawk isn't made for a gunfight," Michael grinned.

"Kinda strange, isn't it?"

"Here? — yeah."

The trees never stirred — there was no wind. Everything was perfect. He imagined it occasionally rained: Snow that would melt as it fell through the clouds of steam.

"No — I didn't mean that," Paul said shaking his head. "What I meant was, well — this whole thing. I mean, walkin' around armed. Fighting just to stay alive. See — you really didn't know it any different. I mean, what's your earliest recollection?"

Michael laughed. "The tooth fairy left me a Swiss Army knife and my mother hollered at my father."

Paul started to laugh. "All right — but I mean — well — I heard that story about you saving Sarah's life when you were just a little guy — sticking that guy — well — "

"The man in the barn," Michael nodded. "I didn't know if I could do it or not. I just remembered Mom had put that boning knife in the duffle bag, and the guy was gonna hurt her and I figured they were going to kill Annie and me too. I didn't really have time to think about it more than that. I'll always remember the look on her face, though. In Mom's eyes, ya know? No—I guess you don't. But I think all of a sudden she realized Dad was right and she had been wrong. Scary."

Paul nodded as Michael looked at him, then, "What are you gonna do? I mean, when this is all over?"

"You mean when we get Karamatsov and there's peace in our time?"

"You're too young to be a cynic."

"I'm older than you are," Michael laughed.

"All right—still. I mean, we will get him. John'll get him. Your dad's gonna make sure this time. He blames himself—he told me—that he didn't put a bullet in Karamatsov's head back there on the street in Athens, Georgia. And it looks like things are pretty much settled with the Germans at the Complex. With Dieter Bern running it, they'll have a democracy, and they should have better things to do than go to war. I don't think we have to worry about these guys," and Paul gestured around them as some of the Icelandics passed. "They're peaceful. Looks like people like you and me are gonna be out of business."

"Dad's planning a clinic, he told me. Maybe I'll follow in the family tradition and learn medicine—if anybody'll teach me."

"Dr. Munchen had to learn someplace. Maybe you can go to Argentina and study there. Madison'd love it."

"Maybe," Michael shrugged. "How about you? What are you and Annie gonna do?"

Paul laughed. "Well—I can't see the magazine business coming back too quickly. I used to read about people like Johnson and Pike and Carson—all the mountain men—when I was a kid. Annie's got a kind of adventurous spirit. I think we might just settle down a while with having children, and once they're old enough, well—" and Paul laughed, "head for the 'high lonesomes'. Should be a lot to explore out there. Maybe more pockets of humanity like this. Things from the past to uncover. I don't know," Paul whispered.

"I don't see Dad settling down with a clinic for more than a little while."

Paul laughed. "Yeah—I'm kinda hoping he doesn't. Wouldn't it be great—I mean if all of us could stay together? You and Madison and Annie and me and John and Sarah and Natal—"

"Natalia—yeah," Michael almost whispered. "One of the movies Dad has at the Retreat is a western called *The Magnificent Seven*—seven isn't such a magnificent number when you're talking about men and women, though. And three's a worse number."

"You know—I mean—maybe I shouldn't say it, maybe I should—but your Dad never—"

"I know that. It's none of my business if he did. I just figure things aren't going to work out that smooth—" There was the sound of helicopters overhead, a public address, the voice German-accented, filled with authority.

"They're early," Paul simply said. "Funny—I'd expected perfect punctuality."

Chapter Twenty-three

Moving swiftly along the slope, their assault rifles slung across their backs, Ladas Kutrov and his two enlisted men gripped only their Stechkin pistols as they moved toward the billowing steam clouds. The heat sources Comrade Major Ivan Krakovski had detected had seemed unnatural, it had been said. There had been a request for volunteers. Kutrov had been the first to step forward. One was noticed by volunteering, and if one stayed alive that notice could lead to things. He had been a captain for a long time.

Kutrov kept moving, the steam clouds closer now, his eyes moving right to left, then looking forward again along the slope. The corporals on each side of him — their eyes looked nervous beneath their snow goggles. The sky that surrounded them, on all sides it seemed at this elevation, nearly a mile high, was gray-blue, heavy, laden with snow, he thought. A blizzard. If a blizzard should hit while he was out here with these two men, there would be no means to return. Death — only that.

He kept moving, running the last few yards toward the lips of the crater opening, throwing himself down to the snow, prone, advancing the few remaining feet on knees and elbows.

He had rehearsed the mission with them in the two

hours that had been allotted before departure. He glanced to his right. Corporal Vilnek was aiding Corporal Kironi in shrugging free of the remote sensor in the special pack slung on Kironi's broad back.

Kutrov looked away, edging a few inches forward, peering for the first time over the edge.

Purple lights. Clouds of steam parting to display them winkingly and then the clouds closing in.

He swallowed. There was life. There should not have been life here.

"Comrade Captain Kutrov—all is in readiness!" It was the whispered voice of Corporal Vilnek, the senior man over Kironi.

Kutrov rolled onto his back, brushing snow from the Stechkin with his gloved left hand, holstering the pistol, then edging away from the lip of the volcano. The camouflage-painted rectangular box—less than a meter square and half that width deep—was already fitted with its white camouflage protective cover, the fiber-optic leads and other sensing tentacles already withdrawn from protective cases, attached with standard needle-fitted coaxial screw mounts to the exterior of the unit. Kutrov helped bury the instrument in the snow, Vilnek feeding out the leads over the lip of the crater, Vilnek's own identical remote sensor still strapped to his back.

It was for implant on the opposite side of the crater if they made it that far—Kutrov looked again at the sky. A blizzard was definitely coming. They had not taken portable shelters, because with the sensors, not really designed to be man-carried, additional equipment had been all but impossible. Kutrov alone wore a conventional field pack containing survival rations, medical kit, other necessities. But beyond these few amenities, there was nothing that would aid them against the onslaught of blizzard conditions in these extreme temperatures. That the temperature had been rising had first alerted him. Then the clouds had darkened, seemed almost to condense.

"The sensing leads are in position, Comrade Captain Kutrov."

Kutrov nodded to Vilnek. "You realize, Corporal— both of you realize—" and he looked into the pale blue eyes of Vilnek, the worried brown eyes of Kironi— "that we shall not make it down this slope alive."

"Yes, Comrade Captain," Vilnek nodded, his face expressionless. "We are aware of the impending storm."

Kutrov nodded.

There was the second sensor to be set. And then, if they made it that far, they would attempt to make it down. They would not succeed, he knew, but to die in the attempt was better than to die without trying.

So much for his promotion to major, Kutrov thought. "Come, Comrades," he said quietly, and led the way down from the cone.

If they could not plant the second remote sensor on the far side of the cone, they had at least to get it as far as half the distance around. Two remote sensors planted ninety degrees apart would get the job done.

He said it again, hearing the sadness in his own voice, "Come, Comrades." And he heard Vilnek speaking into the radio transmitter, proclaiming the first remote sensor to be set.

Chapter Twenty-four

They sat around the conference table, Madame Sigrid Jokli at its head.

Madison Rourke — she thought of herself that way now — was very much impressed and sat with her hands folded in the lap of the pretty dress she had been given to wear, in her mind determined not to utter a word, in her mind the intruder at such a great gathering.

She had watched the women bringing the coffee to drink, bringing the notepads and writing instruments. She would have felt more comfortable doing that — bringing the things necessary for the persons here and then leaving quickly. But Michael had brought her, telling her they had all been invited to attend. She had asked him, "But surely not me, Michael?"

"Yes — you too, Madison."

"But —"

"Put on that new dress and come on — we'll be late."

She had obeyed Michael and dressed and accompanied him. She moved her hands from her lap now to adjust the shawl about her shoulders, her eyes cast below the table, studying her feet in the oddly pretty, very unsturdy looking shoes that had been given her along with the ankle-length dress, the undergarments. She looked up, across the table — Annie was looking at her, dressed similarly, eyes smiling. Madison smiled back. She had prayed to God that Annie would be returned to them safely and Annie had been. Madison had prayed afterward, thanking God for this miracle and for the strength of Father Rourke and of Paul in their quest to find her.

Madame Jokli — a very grand lady and very pretty — cleared her throat and Madison looked away from Annie's eyes, past Michael who sat beside her — Madison — and toward the head of the table.

A tall, good-looking man with hair nearly as long as Madison's own, and the color nearly as blond, sat stroking his flowing beard. His name was Hakon and he was some official from the University where Madison had spent much of the day. Opposite him, on Madame Jokli's left, the opposite side of the table from Madison and Michael, sat Farther Rourke. His hair seemed freshly combed and he had freshly shaved, and for the first time since they had come here, his face seemed relaxed, at ease. Beside him sat Mother Rourke — Sarah, she corrected herself. Between Sarah and Annie sat Paul Rubenstein, his expression blank, his eyes — very dark — thoughtful. He saw her looking at him, she realized. He looked at her and winked. She looked down to her hands again, then up at Michael — his right hand reached out to her, moved across her left thigh, and squeezed both her hands. She smiled up at him. Beside Michael, between Michael and the man Hakon, sat Captain Hartman.

"Relax, Madison." She looked to her right — Elaine Halversen was doodling on her notepad — doodling was a very technically demanding activity, Madison had learned. Sarah practiced this, as did Paul at times. Lines were made that seemed meaningless and then suddenly the lines became a picture. The drawings were not as complete as those painted on the wall of the great conference room in The Place where she had been raised, but they were happy pictures. She was trying doodling in secret until she mastered it and could show Michael the accomplishment.

Across from Elaine, Akiro Kurinami sat, his face, like Paul's face, expressionless and his eyes turned toward the head of the table. Madison looked there too now as Madame Jokli began to speak. "With the arrival of our new friends, the Germans, even more opportunities for the acquisition of knowledge present themselves. And for this, we are grateful. Captain Hartman has spoken by radio with his commander, Colonel Mann, who had in turn conferred with the German President, Dr. Bern, and there is agreement for cultural exchange. This gladdens our hearts, as does the opportunity to learn and grow with our friends led by Dr. Rourke. And hopefully too the Eden Project shall soon be contacted, and with our knowledge of biological science and other skills we have acquired here over the centuries, we can aid these survivors from five centuries ago to turn the North American continent into a garden, a garden of peace. But it is the question of peace that brings us here. As our people of Lydveldid Island rejoiced that we were not alone on this great planet, they were sorrowed to learn that the folly of warfare among men had not ceased."

The doors to the library/conference room opened, one of the serving women holding the doors. Natalia entered. Madison was stunned. "Forgive me, Madame President. I was detained."

"Major Tiemerovna—yes, please, join us," Madame Jokli said. But Madison did not take her eyes from Natalia. Like Sarah, Annie, and Madison herself, Natalia had been given clothes to wear, but Madison had not yet seen her. Sarah looked pretty. Annie looked pretty. Natalia looked like an angel, or a princess,

Madison thought. Natalia's black hair was piled atop her head, but was softly arranged. The long dress and the high waist of the skirt made Natalia's waist seem almost impossibly small, the high lace-trimmed collar of the dress only serving to accentuate Natalia's high cheekbones, the dress's rose color making Natalia's skin somehow whiter-seeming, her eyes more brilliantly blue. The material of her clothes rustled as she moved across the room. Her shawl was folded neatly in her hands, her hands close against her abdomen. Natalia seated herself beside Akiro Kurinami, Kurinami rising, helping her with her chair, Madison noticing suddenly that all the men had risen.

Madison looked again at Natalia — Natalia smiled at her as Natalia arranged the shawl on her lap. Madison wondered where Natalia had hidden her knife and at least one gun — because she knew Natalia well enough now that she knew Natalia would not be unarmed.

Madame Jokli began again to speak. "It is fortuitous that Major Tiemerovna was able to join us, because the subject of this meeting is the unfortunate state of war between the surviving war machine of the Soviet Union and our new-found friends. We have been given to understand that as the Eden Project space shuttle crafts began their return to earth, Soviet military helicopters were waiting in ambush to destroy them. Yet, our proximity to Soviet territory has never once brought us in contact with this military order which we are told rules there. Dr. Hakon Lands and myself would like to put this question openly before all of you."

Natalia stood, her shawl in her hands — she set it down in her chair. "I believe I can shed some light on this. As you know, Madame President, Doctor Lands, prior to The Night of The War, I was an officer with the Committee for State Security of the Soviet, the KGB. I remained with the KGB until shortly before what has been variously called the Great Conflagration, The Fires Which Consumed The Sky. The man whom we discuss here, the leader of the Soviet forces, is my husband."

Madam Jokli, already seated, leaned back heavily in her chair. Doctor Hakon Lands' hands outstretched toward the center of the table. Madison looked from his hands — massive, large-boned, the hands something that instinctively she felt would hurt her if they touched her — to Natalia's face. In a book at Father Rourke's Retreat, Madison had seen a photograph of a doll, the face delicate, exquisite, the eyes wide, the cheeks slightly flushed, fragile-seeming. Natalia was that photograph now, Madison thought.

"My husband is a man of consummate evil. Whether we battle the surviving Russian people or merely battle my husband's forces is the pertinent question here. It seems obvious that he is in a position of vast power with the Central Committee — as I am sure there must be. He has likely promised them the domination of the earth which again likely he thought would merely mean the destruction of the unarmed Eden Project fleet as it returned from its elliptical orbit to the outer edge of the solar system and back. My husband Vladmir is not a military commander, yet he functions as the supreme commander of Soviet forces, it appears. I would say that Vladmir somehow managed to take this underground complex which was built for the survival of the Soviet people and turn it into his personal fiefdom, his military headquarters. I speak only for myself — but I see your world here in terrible potential danger. Should Vladmir Karamatsov somehow be victorious, he will come, and he will destroy you — as he has always tried to destroy what is good and bring war where there is peace." She reached behind her, stooping slightly, taking up the shawl and hugging it against her abdomen as she sat down.

Madison looked toward the head of the table as she heard Captain Hartman's rather higher pitched voice, higher pitched than a man's voice normally would be. But he seemed like a good man, and a competent man. And she had learned one thing since becoming a Rourke: A person was judged by their deeds rather than by some label attached to the person. "Madame President. The Fraülein Major has put the situation most clearly, I think. It is imperative to your survival, your nation's survival, that the Soviet forces under the leadership of the Karamatsov fellow be stopped. My own country sees this as a historical imperative. I propose, as I have been so authorized to do by my government, that your country should cooperate with the German people and the Eden Project survivors, should their leadership also agree, to eradicate Colonel Karamatsov and his forces for once and for all. I am sure Herr Doctor Rourke would agree."

Madison looked at Father Rourke. Father Rourke remained expressionless.

Captain Hartman continued. "To this end, I have been instructed to propose the following: That the government of Lydveldid Island and the government of New Germany agree to the temporary positioning of a military base here that could be used as a staging area against final prosecution of the War with the forces of Colonel Karamatsov. In exchange, totally independent of the already-agreed-to exchange of scientific data, New Germany would pledge to the defense of Lyd-veldid Island against aggressor forces."

Captain Hartman sat down.

There was silence. Madison was pinching the fabric of her dress in her fingers, looking alternately from Michael beside her to Paul, to Annie, to Natalia, to Sarah—then to Father Rourke.

177

Father Rourke began to speak. "Various expressions come to mind—'Times change, people don't'—perhaps that's the best. But perhaps not. Perhaps the best is something attributed variously over the years—'Those who fail to learn the lessons of history shall be forced to relive them'—perhaps that'd be most appropriate here."

Father Rourke did not stand. His eyes were closed and his face turned toward the high ceiling of the room, the ceiling here higher than any she had seen in any of the other buildings in Iceland. "Iceland was spared five centuries ago. Perhaps it was the scientific anomaly it is considered, perhaps a miracle, perhaps both. None of you in this room, with the exceptions of my wife, my son and daughter, my friends Natalia and Paul, and myself can actually remember what the old world was like. And Michael and Annie's memories of it are sketchy at best. Paul lived in New York City—a city in the United States of both unparalleled beauty and unparalleled ugliness, a city in some places given over to savage elements who preyed upon the weak. Natalia lived in many of the large cities of the Soviet Union. And her work, as did my work, took her around the world. Sarah and the children and I had a home well away from any large city, the nearest one Atlanta. But all of us—it was a common sight to see people. How many tens of thousands there may be on earth today—well, there *were* billions. We'd been told for decades that overpopulation might someday prove to be the undoing of us all. Maybe that was true. Too many people. Too many nations. To try to arrive logically at the causes of World War III would consume our collective lifetimes and we might be no nearer the truth than we would be in the next instant. But it seems to me that wars, crime, all the things that humankind seem at once to loathe and yet go out of their way to avoid stopping, are all stemmed from one basic human

178

failing: apathy."

Madison shifted her eyes to Sarah, Sarah in her high-necked white blouse, her hair held back at the nape of her neck with a bright blue ribbon — Sarah's eyes were turned upward to Father Rourke, and Madison saw in them what she saw in her heart when she thought of Michael. Love. Adoration. Father Rourke continued speaking. "It is very easy to say that evil is the concern of someone else. Very easy but very stupid. Evil is everyone's concern. If you are out of its reach, beyond its grasp, it doesn't mean you have no responsibility for stamping it out. The plain facts, ma'am" — he looked now at Madame Jokli — "are these. We will eradicate Vladmir Karamatsov because he must be eradicated. I shot the man once, five centuries ago. Like us — those in my family — he is a living anachronism." Madison's eyes flickered to Natalia — Natalia's eyes seemed tear-rimmed. Her body seemed rigid. Her hands were balled in tight little fists on the table in front of her. "I shot him, thought I had killed him. Each death he brings about is because of my inability —"

"No!" Natalia was to her feet, the shawl falling from her lap onto the table, then slipping out of sight — to the floor, Madison thought. Natalia's hands were still clenched in tight fists — but at her abdomen now, as though something inside her was about to burst and she was trying to hold it inside her. "He's a devil. He is what he is because he's a devil. Inside himself — he had to always be evil. He used his evil, let his superiors in the KGB use it. He's the devil and he wanted to be your God!"

Father Rourke stared at her, Natalia still standing, her body trembling as Madison's eyes flickered back to her. She watched Natalia as Father Rourke almost whispered, "Perhaps that's the question here today.

Will we try to create Paradise or something close to it, or hide, wait—and let Karamatsov rule us in Hell?"

A voice—one she had not heard. It was Hakon Lands speaking and Madison looked along the table, past Michael, toward the man. He stood. "It would seem we have the opportunity to prove that our ideals of these past five centuries have value, have worth. Or, the opportunity to prove that we have no ideals at all, but have merely withdrawn into our philosophy of harmony out of fear. Madame President—I request a called meeting of the Althing at which time it should be proposed that Lydveldid Island join in alliance against this evil. It is only by this means that we can remain true to our beliefs."

Captain Hartman stood, his heels clicking together. His head nodding curtly. "Sir!"

Chapter Twenty-five

The second remote sensor began to transmit a few hours before dawn. Major Ivan Krakovski had instructed that he be awakened.

He sat in the prefabricated shelter, the synth-fuel heater glowing brightly, but he was still cold. Visibility outside the hut was near zero. With the aid of a powerful hand torch and by clinging for life to the guidelines set about the camp connecting hut to hut, he had fought his way against the wind and the driving snow. His body still shook with it. The helicopters had been lashed down hours before. "Word from Kutrov?"

"There has been none, Comrade Major. Only the very weak transmission which stated that the second remote sensor was operational and that the blizzard conditions were intensifying and that the comrade captain and his detail were attempting to make their way down. That was ten minutes ago," the technician said.

Krakovski nodded, watching as the technician returned to adjusting the ball dials for the viewing modes of the remote sensors. The first transmissions from the first sensors had not sufficiently penetrated the steam clouds that filled the inside of the crater of Mt. Hekla. When the steam clouds parted, the tantalizing lavender lights would wink through, then disappear. A civilization—here. It was incredible.

But the transmissions from the second sensor—Krakovski had instructed that the sensor be planted one hundred yards inside the cone and the leads be dropped to maximum depth. And now, as the technician fine-tuned the adjustment, the computer-enhanced fiber-optics images were clear.

Buildings. Greenways. German helicopters.

They had located the Russian helicopter that had been the source of the distress transmissions. There were signs there that a camp had been made, then remade. He wondered—was it the man whose destruction so obsessed the Hero Marshal? Was it Rourke?

The radio operator at the far end of the hut called out, interrupting Krakovski's thoughts. "Comrade Major! A transmission from Comrade Captain Kutrov."

"On speaker," he said dismissively, still studying the fiber-optic image.

"This is Kutrov—Kutrov to forward base—come in. Over."

Krakovski heard the radioman responding. "This is forward base. Reading your transmission. Much static. Over."

"This is Kutrov. One man down—feet frozen. Cannot go on. Second man injured during fall—broken leg and possible internal injuries. Has situation changed? Can we be picked up? Over."

The radioman made no answer.

Krakovski turned to look at the radioman, telling him, "Express my regrets—personal regrets. But to go airborne now would only alert the German helicopter force of our presence. Tell Captain Kutrov that he and his brave comrades shall be remembered for their heroism should they fail to reach safety."

The radio operator just stared. "But—Comrade Major—could not a rescue party—"

"You have my orders," and Krakovski turned away,

refocusing his attention on the screen which showed the German helicopters in some sort of idyllic-looking setting in the base of the volcano. "How are the other sensor readings coming?" he asked the technician, whose short blonde hair was visibly bristling on the back of his neck.

The technician turned to face him. "Comrade Major—you are murdering those men—Captain Kutrov and the others."

Krakovski stood up. He would have shot the man except the possibility existed of damaging the equipment should a bullet overpenetrate. He reached to the technician, hauling the man from his stool, to his feet, the stool overturning, Krakovski backhanding the man across the face, again and again, the man's mouth bleeding, Krakovski throwing the man to the sectioned, prefabricated flooring. The man just lay there. Krakovski glared down at him. "Consider yourself fortunate you are not dead." Krakovski retook his seat. "Now—to your work. I require the geologic profile, thermal readings, the results of the audio discrimination program. Be quick about it." There was, after all, an attack to plan . . .

Annie was sitting cross-legged, Indian fashion, her honey-blond hair to her shoulders, her cheeks tear-streaked. She sat in front of the television, though it wasn't on.

John Rourke saw her there in the recreation room, walked toward her, dropped to his knees beside her, then imitated her posture, crossing his legs. He didn't say anything for a little while. Annie smiled at him.

"What's the matter?"

"Nothin'."

"What's the matter, baby?"

"Nothin'—I told you," she said petulantly, sniffing loudly.

"You're sitting here in front of the TV with nothing on the TV and you've been crying."

"I wasn't crying."

"Ohh—you bet. What's this?" And Rourke daubed his right index finger along her cheek, tracking the tear streak in the dirt.

"Nothin'."

"Sure—tell Daddy."

She looked at him and began to cry, and Rourke picked her up in his hands and settled her in his lap and gave her his handkerchief and she blew her nose hard and it sounded a little funny and he started to laugh and through her tears she started to laugh and she blew her nose again and hugged his neck and said, "I love you . . ."

John Rourke opened his eyes.

He sat up in the darkness, Sarah sleeping beside him.

He looked at the luminous black face of the Rolex Submariner on his left wrist—juxtaposing Eastern Time with Icelandic time, it was four in the morning.

He shook his head, swung his legs out from beneath the covers and his feet to the floor. Naked, he started across the smallish room toward the bathroom at the opposite end from the bed. He raised the lid and the seat and did what he had to do, his eyes already accustomed to the darkness, no need for a light. He lowered the seat and the lid and flushed and walked from the bathroom. He stopped, halfway back to the bed, turned to his left and started for the window.

He drew open the heavy privacy drapes and looked out. The purple lights of the grow-lamp arclights. It made the gardens, the paths, the other buildings he could see here from the third floor of the dormitory-like

184

structure where he had first spotted Annie—all of it—seem unreal. And it was unreal to him.

He opened the sliding door, no one about that he could see, and stepped out, naked, onto the small balcony. He stood well back from the railing, near the sliding glass doors, watching the night that was as bright as the day. In the distance now, from this vantage point, could see the helicopters, see German soldiers on guard near them, the guard only two men, one to keep the other awake, and merely as a precaution.

He suddenly realized he had dreamed.

He hadn't dreamed since the awakening from the cryogenic sleep.

Perhaps his body, his mind—perhaps they were settling back to normalcy, he told himself. It was normal, healthy to dream. And he had been very tired, the conference having moved from Madame Jokli's library at the government house to the University where members representative of the Hekla community in the Athling had been assembled, the matter of the proposed alliance against the Soviets discussed until after midnight.

But again, what Rourke considered reason had prevailed—that to remain neutral was self-deception of the worst possible and most dangerous kind.

There was a knock on the door. He heard Sarah turning over in bed. "John?"

"I'm right here. There's someone at the door. Go back to sleep." he told her, stepping back inside, closing the balcony door, letting the drape fall closed.

The knocking again. "Just a minute," Rourke said, not knowing if whoever it was could understand English. Rourke grabbed up his Levis, skinning into them, zipping them, leaving his belt open. From the nightstand beside the bed, he took up one of the twin

Detonics stainless mini-guns, working the slide, leaving the hammer at full-stand, upping the thumb safety. The pistol behind his back in his right hand, he opened the unlocked door.

The man in the corridor was one of the German noncoms, a face he recognized. In German, the young man began, "Herr Doctor—Captain Hartman has instructed me to inform you that radio transmission signals have been recently intercepted which seem to indicate the presence of a Soviet force of possibly some considerable size to be present nearby. Captain Hartman requested that you come at once, Herr Doctor."

"Where?"

"Herr Doctor? Ahh! To the presidential mansion, Herr Doctor."

"I'll be only a minute," Rourke nodded, closing the door.

He leaned against the door in the darkness, mechanically lowering the safety of the little Detonics, then safely lowering the hammer from full-stand, letting the hammer come to rest over the chambered round as was his customary carry. He settled the pistol into his hip pocket, pushed away from the doorway, and walked on bare feet across the floor to the bed, sitting on its edge. His hands found Sarah, his eyes again accustoming to the darkness.

"Sarah?"

"You were speaking—German, wasn't it?"

"Yes. They intercepted a communication—Russians here, they think, in Iceland."

"Ohh, Jesus," she whispered, sitting up, coming into his arms, Rourke smelling her hair as she leaned her head against his chest.

His fingers touched at her hair in the darkness. "Do you want to come?"

"I'll get dressed."

"Hold me a minute first," John Rourke almost whispered.

Chapter Twenty-six

No one sat—there were too many people filling Madame Jokli's library for that. Madame Jokli herself was still in her nightgown, a massive-seeming shawl almost completely enveloping her as she stood by the fireless hearth.

"It appears that our earlier deliberations were for no purpose. The decision for involvement against the Soviet forces has been made for us if Captain Hartman's information is accurate."

"It is, Madame President," Hartman nodded, bowing slightly toward her.

"In that case? I am open to suggestion."

John Rourke stood beside Hartman. "I spoke with Captain Hartman, ma'am, a moment before your arrival. I think he should share with you his latest data."

"Yes, please," Madam Jokli nodded, her face forcing into a smile.

"Certainly, madame. When the radio transmission was discovered"—Hartman shot his cuff, glanced at his watch—"almost an hour ago, I dispatched one of my officers and three enlisted personnel toward the source of the transmission, prevailing upon Herr Rolvaag of your police force to guide them. There was an undue pause in the transmission, and by acting quickly, the corporal monitoring the radio was able to get another man to one of our helicopters and monitor the transmission there as well, thus forming a crude but effective triangulation. I have just received a coded signal on an ultra-high frequency band the Soviet forces do not seem to utilize. And the message was, in fact, a code as I indicated. It was merely a breaking of an open frequency with a fixed pattern, and thus should be impossible for the Soviet forces to understand even should it have been intercepted. And that condition seems unlikely. Soviet personnel were found. A small force. My men are returning. We should know more within the hour. The message intercepted was *en clair*, or appeared to be so. A distress call from a certain Captain—" and Hartman flipped quickly through the pages of a small notebook held in his left hand. "—A certain Captain Kutrov. References were made to one man of his party having frozen his feet . . ."

"My God," Madame Jokli whispered.

"Quite, madame—and still another man having broken a leg and sustained possible internal injuries. We assume some sort of scouting force. And the possibility exists for electronic surveillance. In previous encounters with the Soviets, some abandoned equipment examined appeared to be remote-sensing devices which might be sufficiently sophisticated to alert a nearby base camp of our presence here. For this reason, I have taken the precaution of keeping activity about the machines to the semblance of normalcy."

"Is there another way out of here?" Rourke turned toward the voice—Natalia's voice. Like Madame Jokli, she wore her nightgown, a shawl cocooned about her shoulders.

Dr. Hakon Lands spoke. "There are tunnels created during one of the eruptions many centuries ago. The tunnels have been explored for quite some time and they are mapped."

Sarah, the only one of the women dressed in other than nightclothes, stepped forward, shoving her hands into the pockets of her jeans. For some reason she reminded John Rourke of some image of Peter Pan—the

189

hair pulled back in a ponytail, the T-shirt out of her pants, her upper body thrust slightly forward, legs taut, spread wide apart. "I think I know what Natalia—Major Tiemerovna—is driving at. Reconnaissance at the least and possibly a surprise attack." Sarah looked back over her shoulder, past John Rourke, toward Natalia, Rourke following her eyes with his.

"Precisely. If some of your people, Madam President, could be persuaded to guide us, a small force might be able to gain valuable intelligence without alerting the enemy that their presence is suspected. And, if the physical situation permits, sabotage, a preemptive strike, perhaps something that could be coordinated with a full-scale strike by Captain Hartman's forces."

"Doctor Rourke?"

Madame Jokli was staring at him as Rourke turned toward her voice.

"Ma'am?"

"Your opinion?"

"Such a small force could be readied pending the return of Captain Hartman's personnel. Unless their information should preclude the use of such a force, I see it as the most logical course of action. I have only one request—if the gentleman will be up to it, I would appreciate our guide being this Bjorn Rolvaag—it would be the opportunity to meet him and personally thank him for saving my daughter's life. And I understand him to be a wonderfully competent fellow."

"Yes. Will you, Dr. Rourke, take charge of this expedition?"

"Certainly, ma'am," Rourke told her. Rourke felt Paul Rubenstein's elbow prod at his right arm, heard Paul groan.

Chapter Twenty-seven

Rourke had showered, re-dressed, and gone to talk with Hartman — the scouts were still not back, but were expected shortly. Walking with Hartman toward the steps of the presidential mansion, Rourke stopped. He had expected Paul to be there, and Paul was, in full battle gear, his Browning in its tanker holster on his chest over his left lung, the German MP-40 submachine gun slung beneath his right arm, his winter gear bunched to a backpack and on the pavement beside him. But Paul was not alone. Natalia, no Victorian-style dress this time, but her "work clothes" — a black, almost skin-tight jumpsuit, high black boots, the black, full-flapped double Safariland holster rig, her hands resting at just below waist level on the flapped holsters that covered the butts of her twin stainless Metalie Custom L-Frame Smiths. Beneath her left armpit, the Null shoulder holster with the silenced stainless Walther PPK/S. The side of her pack, on the ground near her feet, had sheathed to it the massive Randall Bowie knife she had liberated from Madison's former home, The Place. Beside Natalia, staring at Rourke now, stood Sarah, a sweater over her T-shirt, her hair bound up in a blue and white bandanna handkerchief, the little Trapper Scorpion .45 poking out from beneath the sweater at her waist, a Bianchi UM-84 military flap holster set up cross draw on her webbed pistol belt. The rusty, but still perfectly functional, Colt Government Model .45 would be there.

Sitting on the steps, Annie, a heavy-looking dark-materialed skirt, combat boots, a high-necked dark sweater, and as she stood, Rourke could see the pistol belt—they had returned her Scoremaster to her and the Beretta 92-F military pistol that she had told them had been part of Blackburn's survival gear. She wore two holsters now, both pistols. Madison was with her, a rifle leaning against Madison's coat and a backpack, there on the steps. Beside Paul stood Michael, his two mismatched barrel-length 629 .44 Magnum revolvers holstered at his hips, a grin on his face. Michael called out as Rourke neared, "Didn't think we'd let you and Paul go it alone, did ya?"

Rourke stopped walking. "You're not—"

"Well enough to travel, Dad? Wanna bet? Whose son am I anyway?"

"And whose daughter am I—daughters are we?" Annie laughed, hugging an arm around tall, thin Madison.

"It was our idea," Sarah added, looking at Natalia, then back at John Rourke.

Paul shrugged his shoulders, "Don't ask me."

John Rourke simply nodded . . .

Inside the community hospital's emergency room, medics attended the frostbite and injuries of the three Russians, two of them corporals, one a captain. Rourke observed as the man with the frozen feet was examined, saying to Hartman, "In my day, this would have meant amputation."

"Yes, Herr Doctor—but as I understand, not to-day—our own medics and the Icelandic doctors seem to have made remarkable strides."

Rourke nodded, walking from the man with the injured feet to the table on which the Soviet captain was being examined. The man's eyes stared wildly, unbelieving. Rourke began speaking to him in Russian. "Captain—you and your men will come to no harm. Why were you out there on the ice?"

The eyes flickered from side to side, met Rourke's eyes, darted away. The medicinal smell here behind the emergency room curtains was one thing that hadn't changed in five hundred years, still ever-present, still mildly nauseating. One day, Rourke hoped, an agent could be found that would properly sterilize an emergency examination room yet not smell disgusting. Medical science as yet had not come that far. "You can't hope to escape—you're too weak. And you don't have the look in your eyes of someone who would abandon his men and save his own life."

The Soviet captain began to laugh—not the laughter of hysteria, but the laughter of bitterness, it seemed somehow. "Others do these things," the officer said in English.

"What do you mean? You were abandoned out there?"

"It would have betrayed our position to bring in gunships for us."

"I can see that reasoning—hard reasoning, but valid perhaps. Why not a foot patrol? Even considering the weather . . ."

"Yes," the captain smiled, but the eyes were angry. "I don't know."

"Will you give us information?"

"You spoke of things of honor, and you ask for information? Torture me if you like. My men know nothing. All responsibility is mine."

"Nobody'll torture you," Rourke whispered. "Your men—I understand they should be well. I'll have someone keep you informed as to their progress. I think you should do all right too."

The man cleared his throat, the eyes less dilated-seeming. "I do not — do not understand."

"You'll be detained here for a while. But you'll live and be treated humanely. Don't fear — for your men."

"Thank — thank you."

"You bet," Rourke smiled, looking away from the man, finding Hartman, Hartman watching as the third Russian's broken leg was being set. Rourke placed a hand on Hartman's shoulder and started walking him away from the three Russians toward the emergency room doors, saying, "Have someone who speaks English keep the Soviet captain informed of his men's progress. I promised they would be treated decently."

"And they shall, Herr Doctor — under the Leader, when there was SS — it would have been different."

"I understand that," Rourke nodded, clapping Hartman on the shoulder.

They passed through the emergency room doors, Hartman raising his voice slightly now that they were out of the Soviet trio's earshot. "Not far from where those three were found, a rectangular container which my officer was able to identify as one of the Soviet long-range sensing devices was discovered. Wisely, it was not tampered with. From the positioning of the sensor leads, it was presumed that the activities of my scouting group went unobserved. But what is also presumed, based on our testing in New Germany of similar equipment devised by our own scientists, is that such apparatus would be able to clearly show any military activity whatsoever. Because it uses optical fibers and similar types of sensing leads rather than lenses and microphones, it should not be so sophisticated as to detect minor movement and activity. We hope," Hartman concluded, a thin smile crossing his lips.

"All right. Fit us out with radios like your men used in the scouting expedition. We'll signal what we find— and be ready to move in case the opportunity for a strike presents itself. What are you doing about the cone?"

"In conjunction with Madame Jokli's law enforcement personnel—they are rangers, I think, as the word is in English . . .

"Yes—I agree."

"But in conjunction with these men, Herr Doctor, we are moving small units of men with light equipment up toward the cone. We are utilizing the location of the first sensor as our focal point, since we do not know where additional sensors might be positioned. They will work through cover to reach positions that will enable them to guard the cone against ground attack. It will be slow going. Any attempt to discover the locations of additional remote sensors might betray our knowledge of their presence."

"I agree," Rourke nodded.

They walked across the emergency room lobby and into the lavender light outside. Akiro Kurinami and Elaine Halversen were there, as were several German troops and the German officer who had brought back the three storm-battered prisoners. The officers and enlisted men snapped to attention as Hartman approached, Hartman putting them at ease. Another man—one of the green-clad law enforcement officers— was with them, as was Dr. Hakon Lands.

"Dr. Rourke—you wished to meet Bjorn Rolvaag, the man who saved your daughter's life."

Rourke approached the man, Rolvaag a near-giant. Tall, muscularly built, the china-blue eyes visible beneath his flowing hair and above his flowing beard looking as though he laughed at some secret joke. Rourke extended his right hand to the man, Rolvaag shifting his six-foot steel staff to his left hand and clasping Rourke's right hand solidly, firmly. Strength seemed to exude from the man.

Rourke looked at Rolvaag, speaking. "Dr. Lands — please tell Mr. Rolvaag that I am forever in his debt and have no words that could begin to thank him for saving my daughter from death out there on the ice."

"I will, certainly," Lands said, then began speaking in Icelandic, Rourke and the green-clad Rolvaag still clasping hands, Rolvaag's eyes brightening more.

Then Rolvaag spoke, his voice at once thunderous and gentle. Rourke could not understand more than fragments of words where Icelandic and English shared some vague commonalties, but even before Dr. Lands began to translate, Rourke knew the meaning through the look in Rolvaag's eyes, the sustained handclasp: "I was pleased that I was able to help the fine young lady. You are a fortunate man, sir, to have a daughter who is at once so feminine yet so resourceful and tenacious."

No more words were necessary now, and Rourke nodded to the man. It was understood.

They released hands, Rourke turning to Akiro Kurinami. "I wanted you here for a reason. You're very good with edged weapons. So are the personnel of the police force here. But they have no practical experience. I'd like you to try to correct that. If Dr. Lands will help with the translations for you," and Rourke looked at Lands, "you could release a significant number of Captain Hartman's personnel from having to serve as an interior guard."

"I'll do it — yes, John."

"Good," Rourke nodded. And he looked at Elaine Halversen. "I'd like you to work with Madame Jokli. If Soviet troops get inside the crater, we're going to have to be ready to evacuate all noncombatants to some central area down here where last-ditch defenses can be set up. With Akiro coordinating things with the police, and a couple of machine-gun teams from Captain Hartman, we should be able to set up something pretty efficient if the need arises."

"I'll see to it, John. What about you and Sarah and—"

"We're going—with this gentleman, I hope." And Rourke gestured to Bjorn Rolvaag.

Dr. Lands nodded, saying, "All has been arranged. I can provide an interpreter if you wish."

"I think we can get along on hand signals," Rourke answered after a moment. Then he looked back into Elaine Halversen's dark eyes. "We'll be attempting to hit the Russians before they hit us. That storm outside—have you spoken with Captain Hartman's people as I asked?"

Elaine looked to the young officer, telling Rourke, "Lieutenant Baum told me there are moderate winds and the snow is falling almost perpendicular to the ground. From the flake size he reported, considering the wind activity and the direction of the fall—this is only an educated guess because I don't have anything else to go on—but it sounds as though the storm could be of long duration."

"And hopefully they won't go airborne until the storm starts to break," Rourke nodded. "All right—you and Akiro and Dr. Lands get started. Good luck." Rourke returned to Hartman. "You can provide the personnel and machine guns?"

"Yes, Herr Doctor—of course."

Rourke looked at Bjorn Rolvaag. He gestured a "thumbs up" signal. Rolvaag laughed, nodded, and gave a tight jerk to his right thumb, upward.

Chapter Twenty-eight

It was like walking on water, but in some suspended moment of time, John Rourke mused. Waves, but of liquid rock, frozen, the tunnel surface beneath their feet uneven, alternately rough or smooth and slick as ice.

Carrying a torch—why that instead of a light, Rourke did not know—Bjorn Rolvaag, and his huge dog, Hrothgar, marched silently ahead of them, his staff in his right hand, the torch upraised in his left, his heavy outer garments lashed to his pack, as were snowshoes that seemed to Rourke to be better by far than the improvised snowshoes he had fabricated with the help of Paul Rubenstein.

Behind Rolvaag, Rourke walked abreast of Paul, Michael and Madison behind them, and behind Michael and Madison, Sarah, Annie, and Natalia.

There was no talking, nothing to say and, Rourke imagined, a self-consciousness about speech anyway, since Rolvaag would have been excluded from any conversation because of the language barrier. The tunnels were like what he imagined tunnels inside an anthill might be like. Cylindrically-shaped, their angle surprisingly regular for a time then suddenly taking an erratic bend. The rock that surrounded them was a dark gray, the torch smudging the overhead black, Rourke using his own flashlight with the German batteries in it, others behind him using flashlights as well.

He was as heavily armed as practical—the twin stainless Detonics mini-guns, the two Scoremasters, the Python, the Gerber knife and the little A. G. Russell sting IA Black Chrome, an M-16 slung on each side of his body, musette bags brimming with spare thirty-round magazines for the rifles, his Levis pockets packed with loose .357 Magnum rounds for the Python.

Bjorn Rolvaag, although Rourke had offered through Dr. Lands to teach the man the basic operation, had rejected an automatic rifle, carrying only his sword and his knife. Rourke had not pushed the offer of the lightning marksmanship training, because a poorly trained armed man was sometimes at greater disadvantage with a firearm than without it, sometimes as well a threat to those around him. But, somehow, he thought Rolvaag would take well to this. There would always be time later—perhaps.

Finally, Rourke broke the silence, turning to Paul beside him. "When we get out there—I want you to do me a favor. Keep an eye on Michael and Annie and Madison for me. Sarah handles herself pretty well in a fight—almost as well as you and Natalia and I do. But Michael and Annie and Madison are kinda new to this stuff."

"Gotcha. Do we have a plan, or are we really playing it by ear?"

"If we develop any useful intelligence, we can send our friend in green"—and Rourke nodded ahead of them toward Rolvaag—"back with a note. Otherwise, what I'm thinking is we infiltrate the camp and use the element of surprise. Open up on 'em—maybe get one of their helicopters airborne, then call in Hartman's people. According to Hartman, if the Soviet base is anywhere within five miles of the cone, we should have help in under five minutes. No matter how good that Soviet sensing equipment is, they can't have exact numbers, can't know for a fact that the community inside Hekla can only defend itself with swords. If the Russians had been that confident, they would have struck already, regardless of the storm."

"Do you think it's Karamatsov?" Paul asked, rubbing his right first finger alongside his nose—Rourke had noticed this as a habit with which Paul seemed to be compensating for the fact that he no longer wore glasses, no longer needed to be constantly pushing them up from the bridge of his nose.

"Not likely," John Rourke almost whispered. "Probably one of his senior officers. Maybe not even from Karamatsov's camp at all, wherever it is. Might be from the city they have in the Urals."

"How the heck did they know we were here—or did they?"

"I tend to think that the Soviet helicopter Blackburn used had some sort of distress signal. Either Blackburn got to it after Annie stabbed him or Annie inadvertently activated it when she was working to get the radio on. The distress signal might have been very powerful. Who knows who picked it up? But I'd bet that's the reason we have Russian company out there. If it's a large force, we've got real problems. The Germans can't have enough ordnance with them for a prolonged battle and our lines of supply are too long. Chances are, it's a small group of long-range helicopters and a token force. I hope."

"You and me both . . ." Paul Rubenstein murmured.

Ivan Krakovski stood beside the sensing monitors, speaking to the assembled group of officers and senior noncommissioned officers there inside the communications hut. "You have seen the tape of the computer enhancements. This Mt. Hekla's cone is riddled with tunnels, Comrades. By the use of heat-, light-, and sound-sensing equipment, and comparing data with computer models, it seems evident that some tunnels are fully large enough for a small force of men to utilize to penetrate the city, which is in the flat base of the pit crater." Small puddles of melted snow and ice were enlarging about the feet of some of the men, their eyebrows, their shoulders, the skirts of the officers' greatcoats dark with the dampness. "It will be the task of the small force that I will dispatch to penetrate this city, locate the seat of government and seize control of it, then immediately summon our helicopter forces which will be waiting in readiness. Surprise, Comrades. We shall take this Mt. Hekla and from there we shall make systematic aerial surveys of the island, locating and systematically conquering any other enemy positions until all of Iceland is under our control. To the military mind the purpose of this plan is obvious — use of Iceland as a northernmost staging area for the occupation of North America. These people have apparently mastered the control of climate and environment within their city. Such scientific data can be useful to our overall goals of repopulating the earth, enabling our workers and our scientists to survive within even the most harshly cold environments for the extraction of valuable mineral elements, and to maintain outposts everywhere regardless of climatic conditions and prevailing weather. The value of this operation cannot be estimated. I require two officers, two senior noncommissioned officers as well. Volunteers?"

All the men stepped forward.

Ivan Krakovski placed his hands on his hips, allowing himself laughter. "Excellent. Excellent. The loyalty all of you have expressed, Comrades, to the Soviet people whom we serve shall not go unmentioned to the Hero Marshal." And he gestured with his left hand. "Captain Salmonov. Captain Ulyani. Select your non-commissioned officers. The rest of you, Comrades, are dismissed."

Krakovski turned away, to study the current imaging from the sensor which revealed the interior of the crater — all seemed as it had since the first pictures had become available. They suspected nothing. It had been, after all, the best choice to sacrifice Captain Kutrov and his two corporals. A hard choice, but hard choices were often the best choices.

He listened only partially as his captains selected their senior noncommissioned officers, while the re-maining officers and noncoms filed out into the storm.

There would be two penetration teams — to double the chances for success.

"Gentlemen," he said, turning around quickly, "there will be two teams, through the two most likely seeming of the tunnels. Each team will function independently of the other. Should one be delayed, blocked in a tunnel that may have collapsed, the other team will proceed in identifying the objective and seizing the objective. If both teams make it through, again both teams will act independently. In the event of a perfect linking of your teams once you have gotten inside the crater, Captain Salmonov — you will assume com-mand."

"Yes, Comrade Major!"

"Each of you will take twenty volunteers. Equip them however you like from our stores. Utilize a primary radio and a reserve unit. We can leave nothing to chance. If possible, when securing your final objec-tive, keep the head of the government alive to facilitate

202

surrender of their forces. As you progress to your objective, gather whatever useful intelligence data may present itself, segregating intelligence of an immediate useful nature for transmission following the attack signal, maintaining the remaining data for after the attack. Insertion into the tunnel areas will be by means of helicopter which will drop you and your men approximately a mile from each tunnel entrance. After that, you are on your own. Distance through the tunnels, which shall be designated tunnel number one and tunnel number two, are respectively estimated at seven kilometers even and six point three kilometers. Captain Salmonov — you will utilize tunnel number one. Captain Ulyani — you will take your team through tunnel number two. Good luck, Comrades. You have twenty minutes before departure."

He turned away — to look again at his pictures. It was a brilliant operation he had planned, and he was already composing just the right phrases that would discreetly reflect this brilliance for his reports, and, more importantly, for his ongoing history of this final war for domination of the planet.

Major Ivan Krakovski wondered at times if his military abilities which seemed only to enhance themselves, might someday overshadow his literary talents. But he was, as he had often considered himself, evaluated himself, a truly Socratic man, the last of a vanishing breed.

Chapter Twenty-nine

They had paused to rest. The temperatures, as the distance from the interior of the crater increased, decreased. Rourke shifted off his pack, beginning to remove the snowpants and parka that were lashed to the pack. "Daddy? Should all of us suit up?"

"Yeah — I think so, Annie," Rourke told his daughter. "It's not going to get any warmer." As if to punctuate his remarks, his breath steamed as he exhaled.

"We can change back beyond that bend," Natalia supplied, standing, catching up her pack. Madison, Annie, and Sarah did the same, starting back into the tunnel the way they had come, Sarah's and Natalia's flashlights leading their way.

As Rourke donned the snowpants, he glanced toward Rolvaag. Rolvaag was pulling a leather shift into place, over the green cloth shift worn over his shirt and pants. The leather garment in place, he began to remove his boots, substituting for them identical-seeming boots, the linings some type of fleece — Rourke guessed a synthetic, but it could have been natural.

Rourke zipped closed the legs of the snowpants, starting to remove his boots. He utilized special insulated boots for extreme cold and had planned ahead with sizes for Sarah and sizes higher and lower than his own and Sarah's for use by Annie and Michael.

Madison availed herself to one of the odd sizes—he couldn't recall at the moment if she was the higher or lower size. Natalia's cold-weather gear was Soviet in origin, and the Soviet military machine before The Night of The War had been noted for its excellent cold-weather military clothing and accessories, the climate in which many of their operations occurred thrusting this need for excellence upon them. Paul's gear had been "liberated" in a partially destroyed and thoroughly abandoned town through which they had passed between The Night of The War and the fires that had consumed the skies. By treating leather and rubber, and hermetically sealing gear like this, it had remained perfectly preserved throughout the cryogenic sleep. Other items of equipment that could not be preserved in such a manner had been, before the Night of the War, before the activation of The Retreat, exposed to radiation to destroy bacteria and reduce the risks of rot and decay. His equipment would not last forever, he knew, but Wolfgang Mann had already pledged to have additional supplies of ammunition and other necessities manufactured for him in Argentina or New Germany, as Mann and his compatriots liked to call it. One project in which Rourke held special interest was the duplication of the Federal 185-grain jacketted hollow point cartridge that he most favored for his pistols and had always recommended, in the days prior to The Night of The War, in his classes on survivalism and weaponry. Mann had laughingly promised to duplicate the loads, right down to the head-stamps on the cases. Counterfeit seemed to be a more appropriate word.

Rourke pulled on the boots, lacing them securely in place. Rolvaag was resecuring his greatcoat to his pack—perhaps Rolvaag had greater tolerance of the cold, Rourke thought.

Rourke stood, pulling on the parka, but leaving it open, the hood down, the snow goggles and the headcover and the heavier gloves in the equipment pockets of the parka.

He began to reposition his gear—it would soon be time to move out.

Rolvaag turned to him, speaking, gesturing with his hands.

Rourke thought the man intended to scout the tunnel ahead. He looked at Paul, saying as much, then adding, "If Mr. Rolvaag moves out, Paul—you tag along. He's not properly armed for our Russian friends."

"Right," and Paul looked at Rolvaag, tapped the massive green—and now black—clad hairy man on the right shoulder and said calmly, "Me go with you," gesturing with his right first finger to himself, then to Rolvaag, then down the tunnel.

Rolvaag grinned—his teeth seemed perfect and were almost ridiculously white. Rolvaag nodded, catching up his staff, leaving his pack. Paul shrugged out of his pack, grabbing up his Schmiesser and his M-16, then starting after Rolvaag along the tunnel. The tunnel took a bend, and after a moment they were out of sight, John Rourke watching after them, too warm in the parka but too cool without it. He shrugged it down a little from his neck and off his shoulders, Michael coming over beside him. "Where they going? Scouting?"

"Yeah."

"Rolvaag seems like a good man."

"Yeah. How you feeling?"

"Good."

"Stomach all right?"

"Fine. How's that crease on your ribcage Mom rebandaged for you?"

206

"Fine. Looks like your mother's arm's healing well."

"That German stuff is good. What is it, do you think?"

"I think it's some more sophisticated version of some of the products of research into tissue regeneration that were being worked on before The Night of The War. Dr. Munchen explained it to me, but he didn't have quite the English for the fine points. I didn't have quite the German."

"Been thinking."

"That a question or a statement?"

"Statement."

"About what?"

"After—after all this?"

"What you'll do?"

"Yeah."

"And?"

"Maybe a doctor—like you."

"I'd like that. You've got the head for it. The hands for it, too—either surgery or the concert piano. Surgery you could start learning at thirty. You're too old for the piano for anything more than an avocation."

"You play, don't you?"

"Haven't in five centuries. Didn't much before then."

"Learn much music theory?"

"Got heavy into my own composing, but never beyond that. It passed the time."

"Will you teach me?"

"Piano? I'm fresh out."

"Medicine."

"Start you off. The Germans have a top-notch school. You and Madison'll love Argentina."

"What about you?" Michael almost whispered.

"Me? If there's peace, a clinic. If there isn't, it's academic."

"Agreed," Michael nodded soberly. "Wish I had your

experience — for what we've got coming out there," and Michael gestured down the tunnel.

"Don't wish you had that," John Rourke told his son honestly . . .

Paul Rubenstein appraised Bjorn Rolvaag. Taller than John, the physique of a body-builder, the grace of an athlete, silent like the tomb. The dog that followed at Rolvaag's heels seemed like a four-legged version of the man — hairy, huge, quiet, self-confident.

Rolvaag whisked the torch downward and out against the rocks. Paul starting to reach for the bolt of the Schmiesser, feeling Rolvaag's hand against his chest in the darkness, Rolvaag's breath on Paul's cheek as Rolvaag hissed a word seemingly common to all languages: "Shh!"

Paul waited, holding his breath, the darkness total, his ears pricking — what sound had Rolvaag heard?

Paul could hear the dog breathing. Hear his own breathing.

Then he heard the sound, or one like it, that Rolvaag had heard, the clinking of metal. The Soviets, unlike the Germans, still used metal hardware for their slings — it sounded like that. Paul felt Rolvaag's hand gently push against his chest, Paul stepping back from the pressure, realizing suddenly Rolvaag was getting him back, against the tunnel wall.

Paul could feel the roughness of the rock behind him.

Rolvaag's hand left him — Paul heard the breathing of the dog change pattern — Paul felt Rolvaag's hand again, taking Paul's hand, leading Paul's hand to the knife on Paul's left hip. Paul took Rolvaag's hand and brought it to his own chin, nodding his head, to show he understood. They would use edged weapons — but he wondered if Rolvaag understood firearms well enough? But to trust in the total darkness of the tunnels was his only option. As quietly as he could, Paul slipped the snap-closure safety strap of the Gerber, the click sounding like the crashing of cymbals in the stillness, but, he hoped, unnoticed to the advancing Russians. He held his breath—he could hear a cough. Hear a whispered phrase. The clinking of the sling again.

Paul slowly unsheathed the knife, keeping the blade flat against his right thigh, waiting.

There was a sound—and for a moment, Paul thought the enemy had closed with them and he hadn't realized it. But then he realized that it was Rolvaag, drawing one of his own edged weapons.

A light now—Paul could see it, the cone of yellow light growing in intensity and definition toward the exterior of the tunnel, coming toward them.

Paul Rubenstein licked his lips, remembering to breathe again.

If the Soviets had sensor equipment gunshots might be heard—he would try to stick to his knife. John Rourke had taught him some of what Paul had dubbed "the elements of style"—not for writing, but for knife fighting instead.

He waited.

He reasoned. If there were Soviet troops here, their only mission could be infiltration and surprise—which meant they would be no more eager for gunfire than was Paul.

He waited.

The cone of yellow light was nearly full now.

The clinking of slings, the footfalls of men moving not as cautiously as they might.

Paul Rubenstein waited.

Suddenly Bjorn Rolvaag uttered a cry—perhaps a

cry of battle, perhaps a curse. Into the cone of light hacked Rolvaag's enormous sword, the head of the man holding the flashlight severing, falling, the flashlight falling from the dead hand an instant afterward, Paul thrusting himself beyond the cone, at its fringes where the yellow light was gray, stabbing the Gerber into a bulkily uniformed Russian body, a rifle falling to the floor of the tunnel. Rolvaag, his feet visible in the rolling, swirling light of the fallen flashlight — a scream, but the voice wrong for Rolvaag, Paul sidestepping as something heavy, something human, toppled against him — and suddenly as he shoved the body away his left hand was wet and he realized his hand was inside the neck of a human being. Paul jumped back, another movement beside him. If it was Rolvaag — but he could see Rolvaag's boots in the light — Paul stabbed into the darkness, hearing a groaning sound, then diving through the cone of light so Rolvaag would see him. He grabbed at the Icelandic giant, trying to dislodge him away from the light, shouting, "Rolvaag!"

There was a response — and the response was unintelligible to Paul Rubenstein, but then Rolvaag shouted, "Paul!"

"Rolvaag — Paul!" Paul tugged at the man, Rolvaag moving now, Paul running, his hands ahead of him, his knife blade scraping against rock, Paul's left hand finding his flashlight in his pocket — a small Mini-Mag-Lite. He twisted it on, realizing he was running toward the Russians, a Russian face staring at him, a rifle butt hammering toward him. Paul's right hand snapped out and forward, into the throat of the Russian. He snapped his arm back, blood spraying as Paul freed the knife. He turned, running, shouting, "Rolvaag!"

Behind him, he heard shouts, curses. Paul shouted too. "John! Look out!"

Around a bend in the tunnel into another, run-

210

ning—he shot the light back—Rolvaag, his eyes lit like the eyes of a demon, his blood-glistening sword upraised in his right fist, his knife in his left, his staff secured across his back, Russians behind the modern-day Viking, running.

Paul stumbled, caught himself, ran crashing into something—he started to move the knife. It was Michael. "Russians! Watch out!"

A blur as John Rourke dove past him, the flickering glint of steel in the light of the hand torch.

Natalia—Paul smelled her somehow, the warm feminine odor of her, heard the *click-click-click* of the Pacific Cutlery Bali-Song she always carried, heard the sound of steel against leather.

He swung the light—John Rourke locked in combat with a Russian officer, the Russian's rifle bayonet fitted, John Rourke wrestling the rifle away with his left hand, his right hand snapping forward with his knife.

Madison's voice—it was her voice that screamed—at the edge of the shaft of his light, a Russian with a knife the size of a short sword. Paul dove for him, tackling him downward, another body impacting against him. The flashlight rolled across the floor of the tunnel.

Paul grabbed a handful of cap and hair and facial skin, raking the blade across what he hoped was a throat, a hiss, a sigh, the wetness of blood on his hands, the body lurching beneath him.

Paul rolled—Annie, the Mag-Lite in her hand, her other hand holding a blood-dripping knife in front of her. They had simultaneously killed the same man, he realized.

"Madison!"

"Here—all right!"

"Stay put," Paul shouted.

From the darkness—Annie's voice. "I love you, Paul!"

Paul dove into the darkness at a body that smelled of body odor, tackling it, hands suddenly on his throat, his knife pinned beneath him now, the hands loosening on his throat.

The flashlight. Annie—"Let go of him, you son of a bitch!"

She was charging through the darkness, tracking the beam of light. But suddenly the body crushing the life from him was wrenched away, and in the edge of the flashlight he saw Michael, a knife in one hand, his inverted revolver in the other. The knife blade into the Russian trooper's abdomen, the butt of the six-inch barreled Smith used like a hammer, impacting the side of the man's face, snapping the head ninety degrees as the body fell.

Darkness—Annie screamed.

Paul started to his feet, his knife lost, but his hands grasping—a Russian. He could tell from the clothes. "Annie!" Paul tore at the body, falling back with it.

"I'm all right!"

The *click-click-click* sound—Natalia. Paul punched his left straight into the kidneys of the man on top of him, heard a muttered curse.

The *click-click-click* sound—Natalia's voice, Russian—something that sounded dirty. A scream—the scream of a man, unnatural, full of fear.

Paul was to his feet—he felt something brush against him—something soft, but the hair didn't feel like Annie's hair as it touched his cheek. He heard the *click-click-click*—but from far away now. "Madison!"

"Look out—Paul!"

There was a groan, the sound of something hard hitting something soft, a curse, a thud—Paul tripped, a Russian beneath him now. Madison—something in her hands, beating at the Russian's head. Paul found the Russian's face, found the nostrils, his fingers gouging into them as he ripped, the head snapping back, a curse. His left hand found the exposed Adam's apple, the larynx beneath it—his fingers closed together, gouging, crushing into it.

John Rourke's voice. "Everybody all right?"

A light—the Soviet soldier's eyes glaring bright, the light catching in the retinas—and suddenly the eyes were dead and Paul released the grip of his hands, the gurgling sounds something he only realized had been there when they were gone.

Madison—kneeling beside him, her pistol—the Walther P-38 Natalia had liberated from the Place—inverted in her hands, the butt of it dripping blood.

The light moved, to Paul's left—Natalia, her knife still open in her right hand, the long-bladed Randall Bowie in her left, the blade glinting red.

Rolvaag—his sword and his knife buried into the chest of two Russians impaled against the far wall. Sarah and Annie, Annie holding a knife, Sarah with a knitted scarf twisted around the purple neck, more-purple face of a Soviet soldier. Michael—quietly standing, his weapons gone from sight.

John Rourke's voice was a low whisper. "All right—unless we believe in dumb bad luck, this isn't the only patrol. Must be at least one more, maybe more than that, in one of the other tunnels. Natalia—try Russian, anything else you can think of on Mr. Rolvaag—get his opinion if you can. We're going to split up. Sarah, Annie, Madison—you'll go back with Rolvaag—alert the police, Captain Hartman's people—the Russians are doing exactly what we're doing. Do it, Sarah. Natalia, Paul, Michael—the four of us—we'll carry out the original plan. Natalia—get working on Mr. Rolvaag. Sarah—you and Annie and Paul—check bodies with me—anyone who isn't dead, let me know and I'll do what I can for them. Michael—take a flashlight—go up the tunnel—be careful—don't go more than a hundred yards. Whistle three times if anyone's coming. Keep the light out. I'll whistle three times as we come up the tunnel. Hurry!" Rourke turned the light. "Madison—start picking up weapons. Knives, guns, ammo—you and Sarah and Annie and Rolvaag can take 'em back to the crater—extra ordnance might come in handy. Let's move, people!"

The light flickered away.

Paul Rubenstein sagged forward, brushed his lips against Madison's forehead in the gray at the edge of the cone of light. "You're tough, Madison—all right."

"Thank you very much, Paul—you are very nice to say that."

"Right," Paul groaned, trying to catch his breath. He started to his feet—there was no need to check this body. He already knew its condition, his hands the cause of it. He found his small flashlight and went to work.

Chapter Thirty

Michael Rourke flattened himself against the rock—his body shook with the cold. At least, he told himself it was that. Natalia ran up beside him, dropping to her knees, the flat rising portion of the rock not wide enough to give them both concealment.

"A lot of them, Michael," she whispered.

"Yeah," Michael nodded, staring through the steadily falling snow toward the perimeter of the Russian camp. They had trekked three miles from the tunnel, the camp now less than a half-mile away, Michael's body numb with cold, exhaustion. He wondered how his father did it.

"You sound like your father—you look like him, Michael."

"I wish I had his stamina," Michael laughed, keeping his voice low.

"When I first saw your father—it was years ago, a long time before The Night of The War"—She laughed suddenly, Michael looking at her. Her eyes were barely visible beneath the swathing of scarves, the snorkel hood that covered her head almost completely—but she was unbelievably beautiful. His father was made of strong stuff, Michael suddenly realized. "He was very young—your age, I think."

"I'm older than you are," Michael told her, trying to

keep the defensive edge from his voice. They were waiting—his father and Paul would not move out until—he checked the Rolex on his left wrist—until another four minutes had elapsed. There were four minutes to kill. "You're a beautiful woman—I was just thinking how strong my father is."

"He is strong—yes," she nodded, settling onto her rear end against the rock, her M-16s crisscrossed over her thighs to keep the muzzles clear of snow.

Michael looked down at her. "The two of you are alike."

"A propensity for violence?"

"No—superhuman abilities sometimes."

"Training is a lot of it. And there's something inside some people. Your father is the one who really has it. I think you do too—you just have to make sure that it's there. And you will." And her eyes smiled up at him.

"Stubbornness?" Michael suggested.

Natalia laughed. "Part of it—tenacity is a nicer word in English, I think. But it's tenacity coupled with innate ability. Anyway—you'll know it when you see it in yourself, the same way you know it each time you see it in your father."

He looked at his watch, noticing Natalia looking at hers. Two more minutes. Because they were reasonably certain that electronic-perimeter-defense systems would be in operation, the possibility of total stealth had been ruled out. In precisely two minutes, Paul would radio back to the forces of Captain Hartman. Eight long-range gunships. Hartman's force was comprised of four, plus the two his father and Natalia and Akiro Kurinami had flown. The number of men in the camp was impossible to estimate—because of the inclement weather, too many of them would be indoors, inside the prefabricated, dome-shaped shelters that ringed the helicopters.

216

The plan his father had announced was simple. At zero hour, if that was what the moment of attack should be called, they would converge on the base from opposing directions, killing everyone in sight and fighting their way toward the center of camp where the eight gunships were. It would be his job—Michael's—to defend one of the choppers while Natalia got it started. The helicopters were being kept running—that was clear to see, their rotors still but their engines idling, exhaust-gas clouds billowing from them in the cold. Either it was the only way to keep the engines from freezing—which Michael doubted—or they were prepared to move out. This latter choice was the more likely in view of the penetration team they had encountered and fought in the tunnel.

But it would be his job to keep one of the machines clear while Natalia got ready to get it airborne. Paul would have the same job for Michael's father. Once the machines were airborne, Michael knew, his father and Natalia would utilize them against the Soviet machines still on the ground, calling for Hartman to launch his attack.

If it worked, it would take the Russian force by surprise. If it didn't—Michael tried to avoid thinking about that alternative. Madison. The baby she carried in her—their baby.

Natalia spoke. "It's almost time, Michael."

"I know."

"Dark of the moon—they used to say that."

"What moon?" he asked her, smiling. "Don't worry—I'll cover you long enough to get airborne. The trick is getting to the machine."

"It should take us about eight minutes of brisk walking, with this snow and the heavy gear we have and wearing snowshoes—until we hit the perimeter. It could start anytime."

"It starts now," he told Natalia, looking up from his watch.

She pushed to her feet, working the bolts on her M-16s as she started ahead. They would be in cover for the first five hundred yards, rocks, drifted snow against them, grotesque shapes of ice. It was after that, in the open, when it would — he ignored that, working the bolts of his M-16s, walking after her. . .

John Rourke moved ahead on his snowshoes, Paul Rubenstein beside him, the radio message alerting Hartman already sent. Rourke's fists were balled tight through his thinner gloves on the pistol grips of the M-16s, his snorkel hood pushed back to prevent its limiting of his peripheral vision, his eyes squinted through the snow goggles — not against light, because there was little of that, but straining to see each detail of the camp.

Paul Rubenstein was at his left, the Schmiesser — as Paul called it and Rourke sometimes found himself thinking of it — in both Paul's fists, in an assault position.

Perhaps a hundred yards remained of cover, another four hundred yards beyond that when they would be in the open, either spotted visually or by electronic sentry devices.

Rourke walked ahead. He could not see Natalia and Michael, but that was as it should be.

He could see no movement about the camp, except for the wisps of gray-white smoke from the helicopter exhausts. The huts would be filled on a morning like this. When Rourke had last glanced at his watch, it had been nearly eight, and that the camp was not stirring merely further attested to the foulness of the weather. The gray blackness of the sky had not lightened since they had left the tunnel beneath the mountain, and would not lighten, Rourke judged, while this snow fell.

Electronic security would finger them—but he doubted their peripheral system would be more than a hundred yards out. And he doubted that it would be closely monitored. Only someone paranoid would expect attack here.

He kept moving. . .

Annie ran, Madison, her mother Sarah, Bjorn Rolvaag in the "pack" with her. Her mother had advised taking the extra moment to change from the heavy arctic gear to normal clothing and Annie was happy now she had taken the advice. They had run where they could in the tunnel, not daring to risk the radio, and after exiting the tunnel inside the volcano's wall, they had begun to run in earnest, still not risking radio communications lest such communications be monitored by the sensing device implanted by the Soviet troops.

After leaving the tunnel, they had taken the most direct path possible, Natalia having used a mixture of English, Russian, and modern Norwegian to converse with Bjorn Rolvaag. The conversation had been only one way. When Rolvaag would talk, Natalia admitted it had been impossible to understand more than an occasional fragment of a word.

But he had understood well enough to take them along the most direct path now, as best Annie could tell, understood well enough to appreciate the urgency of alerting Captain Hartman and Madame Jokli that the city here inside Mt. Hekla was likely being invaded by Soviet shock troops.

Her M-16s rattled and bumped and banged together across her back, against her pack, her right arm pumping as though it would somehow heighten her speed, her left hand hitching up her skirts, the combat boots she wore, although natural-feeling to her and comfortable enough, still weighing her down as she moved.

She looked at her mother—almost starting to laugh. Her mother was keeping up with her, Madison a little behind, Rolvaag outdistancing Annie and the other two women easily, the dog Hrothgar loping effortlessly beside him.

She told herself it was the length of his stride, and that his sex had nothing to do with his physical superiority of speed. She told herself that, but didn't really believe it.

Running. She judged they had another ten minutes before they would encounter any of Hartman's troops or Madame Jokli's police.

Running. The brightness of the lavender lights was having a psychological effect on her, making her feel warmer than she should have, despite the heaviness of her clothes, despite the run. But she kept at it, feeling her heart pounding near her left breast, running.

Rolvaag—he lurched violently to his right, his staff flailing out.

Armed Soviet troops—three of them were closing on him, bayonets fixed to their rifle muzzles, more of them coming from the high shrubbery on both sides of the flagstone path, Rolvaag's dog going for a throat.

Rolvaag's staff flickered out, clipping one man alongside the head, impacting another in the base of the jaw, both men falling back, his staff locking now against the bayonet-fitted rifle of a third man.

"Bjorn!"

Annie screamed the word, the time for subtlety gone now. The M-16 at her right side was coming forward in her tiny right fist, her left hand moving to sweep back

220

the bolt.

Annie's mother sucked in her breath — not quite a scream — men poured from both sides of the trail. It was Madison who shrieked.

Annie started to swing her M-16 toward Madison, two men grappling with her.

A blur of movement — Annie saw it, felt —

Chapter Thirty-one

They were a hundred yards from the perimeter when the claxon began sounding and John Rourke threw himself into a shuffling run on his snowshoes across the fresh-fallen virgin whiteness that seemed so stark against the gray of the low sky.

Men—some of them without coats—were starting from the huts, broad shafts of yellow light breaking from the doorways now, the snowflakes impossibly large seeming as they formed a lazy curtain within the light, assault rifles bristling in the hands of the men.

The hut nearest him now was seventy-five yards. Rourke didn't fire—each second he bought before their precise position was located was a few more yards, a few yards nearer the helicopters at the center of the compound.

Fifty yards from the nearest hut, perhaps five hundred yards from the nearest of the choppers.

Assault rifle fire sprayed into the snow near his feet. Rourke throwing himself down, throwing one of the M-16s to his shoulder, Paul impacting the snow beside him, Rourke firing a full-auto burst toward the sound of the gunfire, then spraying out the magazine toward the yellow light of the doors. The German MP-40 was opening up in Paul's hands, a furrow of short bursts impacting the snow as Paul tracked toward the target, then longer bursts, men going down.

Rourke dropped the spent M-16 on its sling, reaching to one of the musette bags at his side. Something special he had borrowed from Captain Hartman. Rourke pulled the pin on the fragmentation grenade and counted to five, then hurled it toward the hut, to his feet, shouting, "Come on, Paul!" The grenade went, Rourke stumbling forward slightly, catching his balance, glancing back once as he changed sticks in the M-16—the hut was vanished behind a wall of orange and yellow flame. "Good grenades," he rasped, running on, Paul beside him at the edge of his peripheral vision, changing sticks for the Schmiesser. Rourke had obtained for Paul six extra magazines for the weapon before leaving New Germany in Argentina. They were museum relics there—practical here. He kept running.

More gunfire, but from the far side of the camp now—it would be Michael and Natalia.

The rattle of M-16s, the heavier, flatter sounds of the Soviet assault rifles, more gunfire from M-16s. An explosion—Natalia too had some of the grenades.

Rourke kept running, narrowing the distance to the helicopters by another hundred yards, the camp now filling with men with assault rifles, shouts, the angry screeching of the claxon from the electronic alarms. To his right—a hut door opening, gunfire coming toward him, Rourke feeling impact, but no pain, falling, hitting the snow, his pack. He realized they had hit his backpack.

It was a good pack.

On his side, he stabbed the M-16 in his right hand toward the hut, firing, then to his knees, both M-16s spitting fire, Paul Rubenstein crouched beside him, firing an M-16 as well.

To his feet—Rourke started running again, firing out both assault rifles, letting them fall to his sides on their slings. He tugged open the velcro closures on the storm flap of his coat, then worked the zipper half down, reaching beneath the jacket — the Detonics Scoremasters — he jacked back the hammers, firing.

One gun to his right, one to his left, wingshooting them. A man down on his right, another on his left. The high crackling burp sounds of three round bursts from Paul's Schmiesser.

Another hundred yards gone.

One Scoremaster empty — two more of the Soviet soldiers dead.

Another grenade on the far side of the camp.

Rourke rammed the spent Scoremaster, the slide still locked open, into his waistband beneath his jacket. He emptied the second pistol, doing the same with it, grabbing up one of the M-16s and a spare magazine, buttoning out the spent magazine, letting it drop to the snow as he ran. Another fifty yards gone.

He rammed the fresh magazine up the well, swinging the M-16 right to left, spraying, men going down, left to right, right to left. Another fifty yards gone, the M-16 empty.

A knot of Russian soldiers from a hut to his left.

Paul's Schmiesser was firing, then stopped.

Rourke glanced back — the younger man was ramming a fresh magazine home, running still.

The Russian soldiers from the hut to his left were closing fast. Rourke reached into the musette bag, grasping another of the grenades, wrenching out the pin — he counted to five, letting go, lobbing the grenade underhand toward the center of the running men, the handle popping clear, arcing to the right, the grenade vanished in their midst.

The explosion came, flames lighting the gray sky for an instant, screams, a running man, his body a living torch.

John Rourke had a fresh magazine into both M-16s now. Firing them in tandem, a three-round burst from each into the burning dying man's center of mass.

Two hundred yards to go.

More gunfire and two more explosions from the far side of the camp. The heavy thundering of Michael's .44 Magnum revolvers.

Rourke kept running, Paul's Schmiesser firing again from behind him.

Men to the right — six of them; three kneeling, three standing, their weapons shouldered for aimed fire. Rourke hopped left, skidding to his left knee, his right leg outstretched, shouting, "Paul! Down!"

At the far right edge of Rourke's peripheral vision Paul Rubenstein hit the snow, Rourke opening fire with both M-16s simultaneously now, two men down, a third, then a fourth, the M-16s empty, Paul's subgun chattering, a fifth man down as Rourke dropped both empty assault rifles on their slings at his sides.

He reached to his gunbelt over the waist of his parka, snatching out the six-inch Metalifed and Magna-Ported Colt Python. He double-actioned it at full extension of his right arm, double-actioning it again — the sixth man was down.

Rourke was up, running, Paul beside him. A man running from a hut at their left, a Soviet assault rifle spraying into the snow — Rourke snapped off a double tap from the Python, impacting the man — at center of mass, judging from the way the body took the hits, twisting, jerking, spinning, the assault rifle firing out as the body lurched into the snow.

Rourke emptied the Python into a man coming up at their left, the man's momentum carrying the body toward them, a bayonet fitted beneath the muzzle. Rourke sidestepped, smashing the long barrel of the Colt six-inch across the back of the man's head above the left ear like a piece of pipe in a street brawl, the body going down, Rourke vaulting over it, nearly losing his balance with the snowshoes, running on.

He rammed the empty Python into the flap holster at his side, grabbing a grenade, pulling the pin, looking for a target—eight or nine men—he didn't have time to count—running from a larger hut, firing. He lobbed the grenade toward them, the men dispersing, Rourke loading fresh sticks in the M-16s, spraying them now toward the running men, the grenade exploding, chunks of arms and legs, burning, flying skyward.

A hundred yards now to the nearest of the choppers, men coming from beside the choppers, firing, Rourke shouting to Paul—"Come on! Don't stop or we're done!"

"I'm with ya—God help us!"

Rourke started firing, firing, gunfire impacting the snow around him, a burst clipping off part of one snowshoe as he fell forward, rolled, loosed one of the M-16s, and released the binding. He hit the binding for the second snowshoe, rolling to his knees, firing out both M-16s, Paul running past him now, the loping, gliding run of the snowshoes almost ludicrous-seeming.

To his feet, Rourke dropping both M-16s. He ran, throwing himself into the run, feeling pounds lighter and years younger without the awkward snowshoes, skidding, sliding, running. No time to reload the M-16s, he reached under his coat, first his right hand then his left, grabbing for the butts of the twin stainless Detonics mini-guns in the double Alessi shoulder rig. He ripped each gun free of the leather, thumbing back the hammers, firing, one Soviet soldier down, another down. The nearest helicopter was fifty yards off now.

Paul had fired out the Schmiesser, his M-16 in both hands firing as he ran.

Twenty-five yards, Rourke closing with one of the Soviet soldiers now, firing point-blank into the man's face, shoving the body aside, a man with an assault rifle turning on him, Rourke emptying both pistols into the man's chest, the body flopping back with the multiple impacts.

Rourke wheeled left—a Soviet soldier, making to fire—Rourke hurtled himself toward the man, the force of John Rourke's body shoving the assault rifle aside, Rourke punching both fists against the man's face and head, the fists still closed on the butts of the little Detonics pistols, bloody welts opening on the man's face, the eyes glazing as the body fell back.

Rourke was to his knees now, stabbing the empty and bloodied Detonics .45s into his parka pockets, grasping the dead man's Soviet assault rifle, turning it toward the troops nearest him, firing, hosing the weapon across their bodies until the weapon was silent. To his feet—he could see Paul, locked in combat with a single man—there was no time. Rourke used the Gerber—hacked through one tie-down, circling the chopper, cutting the other three. Rourke ran toward the chopper door, thrusting his arms outward, reaching, grasping at the doorframe and handle, sliding the door open, throwing himself inside.

He looked up and left, toward the forward section of the fuselage—a bayonet was coming toward his face.

Rourke rolled right, reaching to his belt for the big Gerber, the bayonet thrusting toward him again as he backed against the fuselage bulkhead, the Gerber flying from Rourke's right hand. Rourke's left foot snapped up and out, into the crotch of the Soviet trooper, Rourke's right hand reaching under his coat—the little A. G. Russell Sting IA Black Chrome. He had it, the Soviet trooper hacking with the bayonet now, Rourke ducking beneath it, his right arm snapping forward in a lunge for the chest, the little Sting IA biting through fabric, into flesh, Rourke throwing himself down, releasing the knife, on his right side now, his left leg sweeping out and back.

Rourke rolled away, the Soviet soldier crashing forward, his body slamming down over the knife in his chest.

Rourke was up—time to retrieve both knives later.

Rourke ducked, running forward, throwing himself into the pilot's seat, starting to flick switches, his eyes scanning control panels—already the engines were warm, oil temperature and pressure up. It would be seconds before he could start the rotors turning.

Gunfire near the door—he looked back, powerless to do anything if it wasn't Paul—it was Paul, into the doorway, firing, his Schmiesser in his right fist, one of the Soviet assault rifles in his left.

"Haven't had this much fun since I can't remember when," Paul shouted.

Rourke grinned, his eyes going back to the panels— he pulled down his snow goggles, the goggles steaming inside the chopper.

He hit the main rotor control, hearing the reassuring whine, feeling the tremor of movement as the rotor started to turn.

He found his little Detonics pistols, reloading with fresh magazines from the musette bags, keeping the Sparks Six-Pack for emergency loads.

He dropped the little pistols back in his pockets, reloading the Scoremasters now, shoving them back into his belt.

He started the tail rotor.

More gunfire from behind him. "Hurry it up, John!"

"How's Natalia and Michael?"

"All right, I think—I can see Natalia at the controls of one of the machines on the far side—can't see

228

Michael, but I can see men going down as they're charging the helicopter. Must be Michael!"

"Hang on—strap in! We're goin' up!"

Rourke hit the throttle, the helicopter slipping, rising, Rourke slipping it right, across the field of choppers beneath them, setting the machine guns on manual, punching up the targeting screen.

The burping of Paul's subgun.

The helicopter rising to his left—"That Natalia and Michael?"

"Yeah—gotta be—hey—lots of guys running from a hut to port."

"Hang on!"

Rourke let the Soviet gunship spin on its axis one hundred eighty degrees to port, the targeting screen a disjointed blur, then the bulls-eye settling. Rourke shifted it over the pack of fifteen or so men running for the helicopters. He worked the fire control, opening up, furrows cutting into the snow, advancing toward them, impacting their bodies, the bodies lurching right and left, falling.

Paul Rubenstein's voice. "This is Rubenstein. Rubenstein to Hartman! Attack! Attack! Acknowledge. Over!"

There was a crackle of static, then Hartman's voice. "This is Hartman—message understood. Will comply. Hartman out!"

Natalia's gunship was fully airborne now, a missile launching from the starboard rack, then from the portside rack, one of the Soviet helicopters gone, one of the huts bursting into flames.

More helicopters were starting off the ground now. Two. Three. Four—Rourke switched to missiles, dismissing the machines going airborne for a moment, targeting the last of the machines on the ground, activating the fire control, the helicopter jerking a little as his eyes followed the contrail of the missile from the port-side rack — the helicopter was there on the ground one instant, then engulfed in a ball of flame and smoke the next.

Rourke glanced through the chin bubble — one of the Soviet helicopters coming up, dead for them.

Rourke banked the machine hard starboard, arcing away from it, another of the gunships closing with him, ground fire impacting the helicopter's undercarriage, pinging off the armor.

Assault rifle fire from the rear of the fuselage, and Paul's M-16 answering it.

Rourke came out of the starboard bank, banking now to port, his stomach lurching with it as he scanned for a target, settling his missile-target grid, punching fire control — one of the Soviet gunships blew out of the gray sky, debris, burning, raining down toward the ground as Rourke banked to starboard, the bubble scorching around him, Paul shouting, "Shit, that was close!"

"Only counts in horseshoes — stay back — we might do that again. Never know." Gunfire — it chiseled across the port side of the chin bubble, then laced upward, Rourke banking the machine away from it.

The contrail of a missile, right past him, the missile spinning off, exploding in the distance. Machine-gun fire. Rourke switched to machine guns, climbing, the heavy machine-gun fire impacting the helicopter's tail section, Rourke starting to lose control of the tail rotor. "Shit," he snarled, changing rotor pitch and starting down, nosediving toward the gunship that had hit him.

His machine gun — Rourke settled the grid, the enemy gunship taking evasive action.

Rourke punched up missiles, firing — one port, one starboard, flanking the enemy gunship on either side — the evasive action ceasing as Rourke hit the fire control

230

on his machine guns, aiming for the center of the bubble, sweeping up and across the machine's dorsal side, Rourke changing pitch, banking slightly to starboard, crossing over the enemy gunship, firing into the main rotor now, the machine exploding beneath him.

He could see Natalia's machine—he had memorized the fuselage number, the only way to identify it.

She was firing missiles into the huts beneath them now.

In the distance, coming over the cone of Mt. Hekla, the black wasp shapes of the German helicopters. He could hear Hartman's voice breaking the static from Paul's radio. "We have visual contact and are closing. Give your fuselage numbers."

"Damn," Rourke hissed. "Paul—read 'em Natalia's numbers—quick."

He could hear Paul, giving the numbers. Then Hartman's voice. "Herr Doctor Rourke's numbers?"

"What's our number, John?"

"I don't know—tell him to count to five and when he does, I'll fire a missile due south."

Paul repeated as Rourke started climbing, hitting his missile control, the tail rotor still making control difficult. He could hear Hartman's voice now. "One. Two. Three. Four. Five."

"Paul—tell him *two* missiles, in case we were intercepted. Now!"

Rourke fired one port and one starboard off his racks, due south, Paul's voice as the chopper shuddered. "Make it two missiles, Captain."

"We have you, Herr Rubenstein—stay back now!"

The German choppers were closing.

Rourke swung his own machine one hundred eighty degrees and fired his machine guns toward the huts, starting a strafing run.

One of the Soviet choppers was getting away and

231

Rourke changed direction, starting to pursue.

"Hey—John! I smell smoke—holy shit!"

It was the tail rotor—Rourke could see it on the emergency controls—they were on fire.

"Hang on—going down!" Rourke glanced once more toward the fleeing chopper. He could feel it inside him—it wasn't Karamatsov.

That was still to come.

Chapter Thirty-two

When compared side by side in battle, the Soviet machines had armor inferior to that of their German counterparts, and the avionics were not as good either. The Soviet helicopters had been designed, it seemed, with total uniformity in mind, the German machines designed to allow the individual pilot to excel.

The Soviet chopper was burning a few hundred yards behind them, as Paul Rubenstein and John Rourke moved about the abandoned encampment, Rourke recovering his knives as they left the machine. The destruction was almost total and Rourke doubted any useful intelligence data could be gleaned from here. Two German helicopters had gone off in pursuit of the Soviet chopper that had fled, but Rourke doubted they would catch it. The typical modern Soviet command policy, he had learned since the return of the Eden Project, was to plan for command survival at the expense of screening actions that expended the lives of subordinates unnecessarily.

It had been that case here.

One of the German helicopters was starting to take off, Hartman running across the snow toward them, slipping, catching himself, running, waving his hands toward them.

Rourke looked at Rubenstein—"Come on—I think something's up," and Rourke broke into a skidding dead run to link with Hartman, Paul Rubenstein beside him.

"Herr Doctor," Hartmann was shouting. "Herr Doctor!"

Hartman stopped, Rourke and Rubenstein meeting him midway across the gutted base camp site. "A team—a team of Soviet commandos—they have penetrated the presidential residence, using hostages to force their entry."

"Hostages—"

"Your daughter. Your wife. Your son's wife. One of the police—Rolvaag—"

John Rourke started to run, toward the nearest of the German machines—overhead, he could see Natalia's Soviet aircraft. Michael was aboard it still. It was speeding toward the volcano. . . .

Annie Rourke sat with her hands in her lap, watching the Russian officer as he paced. His men were in positions at each of the library windows, thus dominating one half of the lower floor of the presidential palace. She knew enough about tactics that the position was indefensible, except for the fact that they held hostages. Her father's library had held considerable data about the operation procedures of such groups as the British Special Air Service, the Navy SEAL Teams, and the like. If there had not been hostages and a prolonged shootout were to be avoided, a team of men could simply have come through the ceiling from the floor above them, timed with an assault through the library doors. Gas, perhaps, if such things as sound and light grenades still existed, these too.

But the hostage situation was the problem—in a strange way, she was almost glad she was on the inside as a hostage rather than on the outside as someone trying to solve the tactical problem. It seemed insoluble. She had considered the fact that she might well die this time.

Her head still hurt — a rifle butt against her neck, she supposed. Considering that, she also supposed she was lucky to be alive. For the moment.

The Soviet officer spoke English, oddly accented but sufficiently fluent. He had been polite enough.

He had told them there was no reason for the four women to be forced to be uncomfortable — Madame Jokli had ordered him from her house. He had asked to be forgiven for the inconvenience caused her.

The four women had been placed in four of the conference-table chairs and ordered to remain seated and to remain quiet, and had been told that if they complied they would remain unmolested.

Her mother sat to her left. Madison sat to her right, Madame Jokli behind her. Annie had a view of the library doors and grew weary of looking at them — she had begun counting studs in the ornamental chair molding that ran the length of the wall on each side of the doors between the bookcases.

Only poor Bjorn Rolvaag was tied up. His dog howled from somewhere outside. When she turned her head left, she could see Rolvaag in the far corner, hands and feet bound, the ankles drawn up almost to his wrists, a noose about his neck lest he snap the rope binding ankles to wrists. The motion, were he to try it, would break his neck.

There had been no gunfire from outside the building since the initial fire-fight when they had entered. Three of the Soviet captain's men — his name had been given as Salmonov — were dead outside, leaving nineteen, including himself and a senior non-commissioned officer. Of the nineteen, two were wounded, but their wounds bandaged, they still seemed fit enough to fight. The dog, Hrothgar, had accounted for one of the

235

wounds.

And suddenly she heard her father's voice, "This is Dr. John Rourke. You are holding my friends against their will." Friends? Of course, she realized — Salmonov wouldn't know he held John Rourke's family, and the information would only make him more careful of his prize. Her father's voice, over a PA system, went on. "I'm coming inside to discuss some resolution to this situation. I'll be armed, as I have no desire to be taken hostage as well. This message will be repeated by a person here who speaks Russian, should you not have understood. When she concludes, I'll enter."

There was a flurry of movement and she turned her head toward the windows overlooking the greenway, a harsh-sounding Soviet voice shouting, *"Nyet!"*

She returned her gaze to the front. The second voice began with the Russian translation. She recognized the voice as Natalia's.

Her father was just going to walk in here.

Her father's voice again, saying, "I'm coming inside in sixty seconds. There's no need to shoot. I want to talk." Natalia's voice again, repeating, Annie assumed.

Salmonov ran to the library doors, his senior non-com with him, other men as well, besides the three already at the doors.

Salmonov turned toward her and the other women. "You will remain seated, perfectly still. I have heard of this Dr. Rourke, one whom our Hero Marshall wishes to kill. When this Rourke enters, we will talk. Then I will take him prisoner. Say nothing, or all of you will die. Once I have him, I will not need you any more. Remember — total silence — look straight forward!"

He turned away — Annie's fists bunched the material of her skirt.

Her father was walking into this — did he expect that she and her mother and Madison perhaps would be able to help?

She began, without moving her head, to shift her gaze — the nearest of the Soviet soldiers was ten feet away. Not a burly man — she thought she could take him if she did it quickly.

Her father would get their attention — for an insertion through the ceiling? for an assault toward the window positions?

Paul — he would be ready — Natalia. Michael — but for what? she asked herself.

She realized that since only she faced the doors, any action that her father might subtly signal would be dependent on her interpretation.

Annie Rourke began forcing out other thoughts, began focusing her attention on the doors, to shift it to her father's face, to his eyes, to his words, his body language. He would be counting on her or her mother to read him, to react.

There was a knock at the doors.

Salmonov and the others stepped back, the senior noncom working the handles. Then he too stepped back.

Annie shifted her head slightly to the right to see the center of the doorframe, past Salmonov's shoulders.

The doors opened, her father filling the opening, his head nearly as tall as the doorframe's crosspiece.

He wore his double shoulder holsters with the little Detonics pistols, his Scoremasters in his belt — she noticed the hammers of the Scoremasters were cocked. She couldn't tell if the little .45s were cocked. But he never carried cocked, he had told her once, never cocked and locked unless trouble was immediately imminent.

Annie Rourke licked her lips.

Her father spoke. "Thank you? English?"

"You will surrender your weapons, Dr. Rourke."

John Rourke didn't move. His voice was low. "No — I came to talk. We do that first."

Salmonov laughed. "Very well, Dr. Rourke — talk if you must. But you shall not leave."

Her father shrugged his shoulders — Annie tensed. She studied his hands — the fingers were slightly curved, flexing a little as his hands hung loosely at his sides, but the elbows were slightly cocked to prevent any loss of circulation.

"Your base camp was completely destroyed. Only one helicopter escaped. I presume your commander was aboard it. You are cut off, thousands of miles from assistance. If you surrender your hostages now, I give my pledge that you will be treated with dignity and allowed to sit out this war in relative comfort, and after it is through, return to your families. If you do not surrender, regardless of what demands you make, they will not be met. You will all die. I guarantee that. The decision is yours, Captain, yours and your men's. I said my piece."

His eyes didn't flicker.

His hands didn't move.

Salmonov spoke. "We of course refuse to surrender, Dr. Rourke. Our demands shall be forthcoming. But, I advise that you surrender, or otherwise these innocent hostages might well come to harm. I will take your guns, sir."

Because of the angle at which her chair had been placed, she could see past Salmonov, could watch her father.

She knew what was happening now, knew her mother would know. She felt her shoulders tense. She wiggled her toes to get circulation going in her legs. She was ready.

Her father's hands slowly moved to his waistband, slowly withdrawing the big Detonics Scoremasters.

Her father's hands swathed the pistols, despite their size, the butts of the cocked .45s presented toward Salmonov. He said, slowly, softly, his voice little over a whisper, "You're making a mistake, sir."

Salmonov laughed.

The timing would have to be perfect, Annie knew.

She heard the clicks of the safeties, saw the blurring motion of her father's hands, shouted, "Mom—get Madame Jokli down!" Already, as the twin blasts from the .45s began to ring in her ears, she threw herself right and back, grappling Madison from her chair and to the floor, forcing Madison's head down—but she couldn't draw her eyes from her father's hands. As Salmonov fell, the pistol in his right hand discharged, the top of the noncom's head blowing off in jagged chunks; the pistol in his left hand, his arm stabbing straight outward, firing—the soldier who had been ten feet away from her going down, his nose shattered, globs of blood pouring from it, spraying. The pistol in his right hand—a soldier near him who was raising an assault rifle. The pistol in his left hand—another of the soldiers by the door; the pistol in his right hand—the third soldier who had been at the doors as a guard. The pistol in his left—a soldier near the library windows, the body rocking back, shattering through the glass, outward, as the other library window shattered inward, Paul's body coming through in a roll, his Schmiesser firing now.

The pistols in her father's hands barked simultaneously—another soldier down, the man's assault rifle turning toward Annie and Madison, discharging into the floor near her as Annie closed her eyes. The booming of her father's .45s—again and again. Her eyes opened.

Natalia, jumping through the already-shattered window through which the guard had fallen, her revolvers blazing from each hand.

Her father was moving across the room now, in a long-strided walk, the Scoremasters gone from his hands, the little twin stainless Detonics mini-guns replacing them, firing.

Michael—he was through the doorway her father had entered by, his .44 Magnum revolvers bone-shatteringly loud as they barked from each hand.

Screams—bursts of assault rifle fire—still she could not take her eyes from her father.

Both pistols stabbed outward, at point-blank range discharging into the head of one man—his left eyeball, the entire left side of his face seeming to disintegrate— the neck of another.

She heard the *click-click-click* of Natalia's knife as Natalia approached the trussed-up figure of Bjorn Rolvaag.

The gunfire ceased.

Her father, his pistols in his hands, his hands at his sides, walked across the room—toward her as she rose to her knees, then to her feet. Madison—she helped Madison up. Her mother—her mother was standing, helping a glassy-eyed Madame Jokli to her feet. Michael ran across the room, sweeping Madison into his arms. Annie turned around—Paul—he took her in his arms, kissed her, held her tight—but still Annie Rourke could not take her eyes from her father. His pistols still in his hands, he folded her mother into his arms, his eyes scanning the room as if searching still for danger.

Her father.

No one was like him, Annie Rourke knew.